CAPTAIN CORELLI'S
MANDOLIN

The Illustrated Film Companion

CAPTAIN CORELLI'S
MANDOLIN

The Illustrated Film Companion

Steve Clark

Introduction by
Louis de Bernières

Written by Steve Clark

Diary extracts by kind permission of Kate Iakovatou-Tool

First published in 2001 by
HEADLINE BOOK PUBLISHING

10 9 8 7 6 5 4 3 2 1

British Library Cataloguing in Publication Data is available from
The British Library

ISBN 0 7472 3770 0

Printed and bound in Great Britain by Bath Press Colourbooks, Glasgow

Designed by Isobel Gillan
Stills photography by Peter Mountain
Watercolour sketches by Jim Clay
Work on film graphics by the Printed Word

Headline Book Publishing
A division of Hodder Headline
338 Euston Road
London NW1 3BH

www.headline.co.uk
www.hodderheadline.com

ACKNOWLEDGEMENTS
The author is indebted to everyone who helped with the preparation of this book
(alphabetically): Sergio Albelli, Rea Apostolides, Mick Audsley, Christian Bale, Tim Bevan,
Charlie Bodycomb, John Bohan, Lois Burwell, John Bush, Alexandra Byrne, Nicolas Cage,
Diane Chittell, Tania Clarke, Jim Clay, Richard Conway, Penélope Cruz, Jim Dowdall, Paul
Englishby, Federico Fioresi, Francesco Guzzo, John Hurt, Carrie Johnson, Steve Lamonby,
Salvatore Lazzaro, Olivia Lloyd, John Madden, Piero Maggio, Germano di Mattia, David
Morrissey, Irene Papas, John Parichelli, Kathryn Perkins, Davide Quatraro, Paco Reconti,
Quinny Sacks, Chris Seagers, Mary Selway, Nuccio Siano, Shawn Slovo, Richard Smedley,
Simone Spinazzè, Sandro Stefanini, Anna Stock, Susie Tasios, Lisa Tomblin, James
Wakeford, Stephen Warbeck, Joan Washington, Lisa Williams – and especially to Kevin
Loader and Sarah Clark. Of particular help as a source of historical reference was *Military
Advisor* (R. James Bender Publishing). Thanks also to my agent Sheila Ableman and to
Doug Young, Lorraine Jerram and Jo Roberts-Miller at Headline Book Publishing.

CONTENTS

Filming locations on Cephallonia

1 **Horgota Beach:** Used as setting for Mandras's beach. Mandras is seen fishing from his boat; Corelli and Pelagia part; Mandras seen leaving the island. The hill above was used when Pelagia runs towards the beach. The jetty was used when Pelagia is playfully thrown by Mandras into the sea.

2 **Sia Monastery:** Where Pelagia and Corelli's love scene was shot.

3 **Myrtos Beach:** From the cliff above, locals watch Corelli prepare to explode the mine; Corelli inspects the mine on the beach; Weber meets Corelli; and the La Scala boys cavort with the Italian prostitutes.

4 **Sami:** The set built around the Kastro Hotel to portray wartime Argostoli. Argostoli main street: Italians arrive; Corelli and his men make their way to the harbour with their gun; battle scenes between the Italians and the Germans. The waterfront: Italian soldiers disembark. The party: Pelagia dances with Italian soldier. The square by the Kastro Hotel: audience watches newsreel of Germany invading Greece; surrender of town hall.

5 **Antisamos Beach:** Italian encampment; Carlo arrives and meets Corelli in the latrines; Corelli drills his men; 105 gun is on a bend in the road on the headland above.

6 **Dihalia village:** Dr Iannis's house was built on the top of this village which was ruined by the 1953 earthquake. Sets include: Drosoula's house; village main road: where the villagers watch the Italian convoy pass; village square (including the *kapheneion* and the church): where Mandras enlists; Corelli plays Pelagia's Song; Mandras ties Pelagia's skirt to the chair.

7 **Old Vlachata, Karavomylos:** Walled yard: the firing squad scene. Deserted farmhouse: Mandras asks Corelli for arms. Mountain retreat: Corelli and the partisans unload arms and ammunition. Country road: nuns lead the mentally disturbed towards the village.

8 **Mount Aenos:** Ambush road: the Germans set up a roadblock and the Italians surrender their guns; Mandras and partisans blow up German convoy.

9 **Kaligata:** Argostoli suburbs: where Corelli and his men travel towards battle.

10 **Karamies:** Country roads where Corelli and his soldiers travel in trucks.

11 **Ag Fanentes Monastery:** Captain Corelli returns; village feast, singing and dancing; Velisarios fires the cannon; Father Arsenios intones over the body of the saint; the villagers witness a miracle.

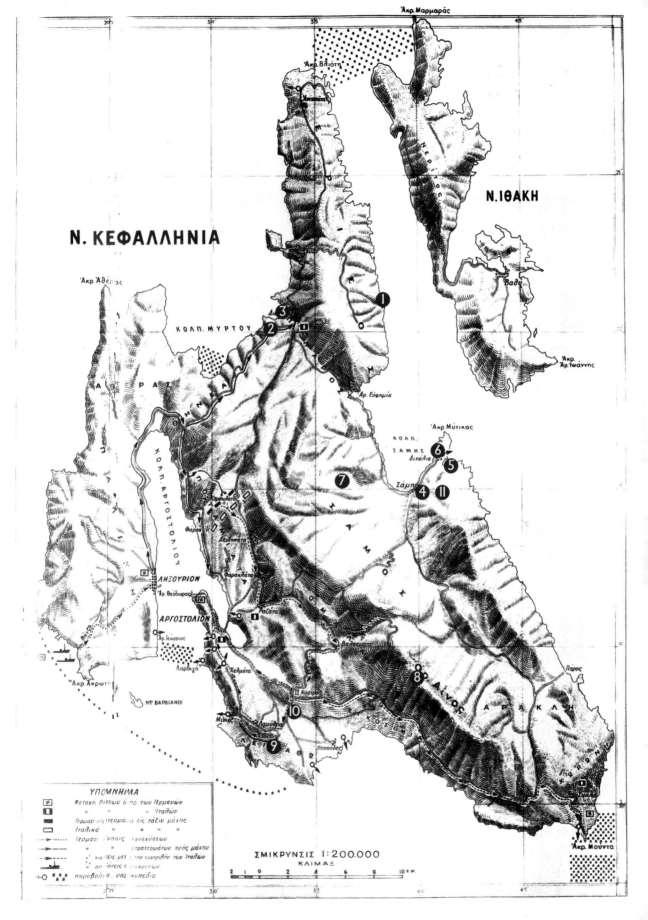

INTRODUCTION

by Louis de Bernières

I have always noticed that after publishing a book, people inevitably ask, 'Is there going to be a film?' They ask this question in tones of great excitement, with a slight widening of the eyes. I am left with the suspicion that most people think that a film is far more wondrous than a novel, that a novel is, perhaps, just a hopeful step in the celluloid direction, and that if there is no film, then the author has partially failed. It is as if 'the film' confers a mysterious super legitimacy upon the writer's work. Objectively speaking, of course, a film's relation to a novel is as a charcoal sketch to an oil painting, and no writer I know of would actually agree that 'the film' is the ultimate aspiration. Certainly, any literary novelist who deliberately tried to write something tailor-made to appeal to film-makers would fail to produce a good book, because the fact is that books are only filmic by accident.

It is in any case a long journey from page to screen, because the first stage involves 'selling the option', whereby, in return for a modest sum, and for a limited time, a producer retains the right to be the first to have a bash at making the film, should he get round to it. It is theoretically possible to go for decades having the option renewed, with no film being made at any time at all. This is money for jam, of course, but the sums are not big enough to be truly conducive to contentment. My first novel had the option renewed several times, and then finally it was dropped. This is, alas, a common fate, and many a novelist remembers all those little bursts of hope with a wry smile.

In the case of *Captain Corelli*, however, the book eventually made it over the real hurdle, which is the exercising of the option. This is the point where a more substantial fistful of cash changes hands, but regrettably even this is not enough to meet the expectations of loved ones and acquaintances, who strangely assume that you are imminently to be stinking rich forever and can afford to buy them a yacht each for all their birthdays for the rest of their lives.

More importantly, here begins the battle that inevitably takes place in the author's psyche thereafter. The hard fact is, that it is no longer one's own book. Roger Michell and Kevin Loader did ask me if I would like to do the script, and no doubt they were mightily relieved when I declined. Novelists, you see, rarely make good script-writers, and in any case I couldn't have taken the job

John Hurt as Dr Iannis
at the Feast of
St Gerasimos

on without being a hypocrite – I had often told off my good friend, Esther Freud, for wasting literary energy turning her novels into scripts when she should have been writing more novels. She has had the experience of doing numerous drafts, and then finding that her scripts are still not used. I wasn't going to put up with that, because I have the natural arrogance of most literary writers, which she unaccountably lacks. As far as I am concerned, once I have written something, then that is the way it must be, it is perfect, and no one is going to make me change it. Script-writers have to be humble creatures who *will* change things, and even knowingly make them worse, a thousand times and a thousand times again, promptly, and upon demand. I would rather be boiled in oil. In fact, I would almost rather go back to being a schoolteacher, and there can't be anything worse than that.

It is, as I say, no longer your own book. The director has the right to make any changes that he fancies, and so your carefully crafted (non-autobiographical) novel about serial adultery in Hampstead can end up being set in Manhattan, involving a car-chase, a roof-top shoot-out, and abduction by aliens. This, from the writer's point of view, is the real horror of film. I cannot count the number of people on the set of *Captain Corelli's Mandolin*, who, *à propos* of possible changes to the story, repeated to me in a serious tone that 'Of course, film is a completely different medium'. This mantra is solemnly repeated so that film-makers are self-absolved from any irritation that may be set up by altering the story or the characters. I think that it is really a cliché which is either untrue or too vague to be meaningful. There could not be anything simpler than extracting the salient points of the main narrative, and making a faithful film, which is what all readers and writers would actually prefer. My theory is simply that film-makers are hell-bent upon a bit of territorial marking, and each time one can only hope that they have sufficient genius to do it with flair. There are, after all, a few films that really are better than the book, and it would genuinely cause me no distress were people to say this of *Captain Corelli's Mandolin*.

All I was able to do in order to ensure that *Captain Corelli's Mandolin* would be treated respectfully, was to insist to my agent that the book should not be sold to Hollywood. I wanted it made by a European company, and so when Working Title made an offer for it, I decided that this was exactly the right way to go. There was then a dodgy moment when the original director, Roger Michell, had to drop out for reasons of health, a crisis which was resolved when the equally gifted John Madden accepted the job. He was obliged to come into the project after it had already undergone very considerable development, a most unenviable position in which to find himself.

I must say that I was most impressed by my visit to the set. It was obvious to me that everyone was going flat out to produce a classic, and apparently enjoying themselves in the process. It was a happy place. On the first day, I encountered Tim Bevan, one of the producers, sitting on the seafront wall, and didn't recognize him because he looked like a fisherman. Everyone had been seduced by Cephallonia, and this compensated for the frustrations caused by having to deal with local officials and the risible nonsense printed in both the Greek and the international press.

The set itself was so good that I couldn't believe it was not the real thing. I thought, until I walked behind and saw the wooden scaffolding, that they really had rebuilt old Argostoli on the front at Sami. One campanile was painted so cleverly that I lost a bet over it, believing it to be three-dimensional when it was really flat. The trouble that had been taken to get everything right must have been immense, and this was borne out by the fact that old people were bringing their grandchildren in order to show them what the island was like before the earthquake, and that coaches were arriving, full of schoolchildren. Ships were disguised as wartime ones, and Russian motorbikes masqueraded with complete confidence as German BMWs. It was an *Alice In Wonderland* experience to be wandering about in shorts with a camera, in the midst of a world that was, so to speak, an authentic illusion of Cephallonia as it was sixty years ago.

Italian forces await an official surrender from the Cephallonian authorities

Next to the set, the most impressive thing was seeing how painstaking the actual process of filming is. Everyone is perfectly prepared (if not happy) to stay up all night for several days, in order to get the best version of a scene that might take up only a minute in the final cut. For me it was a salutary lesson to witness such perfectionism, and it made me realize how lucky I was to be in a branch of the arts that does not require such co-operation, endurance, and grinding hard work.

I remember once being made to walk up my garden path again and again by a Canadian film crew making a documentary in which I was to be featured. I had to stop and pick a piece of mint, and then carry on up the garden path. After doing it ten times I lost my temper, much as I did when once a features editor asked me to rewrite an article three times. I am not, I think, morally or temperamentally suited to being in film, and I was both horrified and deeply impressed by how willing and compliant John Madden's army was.

What was most astonishing, perhaps, was that everyone put their utmost into every take, as if each were the first, and as if they were all fresh. It was somewhat magical to see Penélope Cruz repeatedly dancing her way through one scene, without any perceptible diminution of creative energy or good humour at all. I have to say, though, that for the observer the interminable and apparently indistinguishable repetitions eventually become excruciatingly boring, and I decided that if I were ever to make a film I would probably not allow myself more than three goes at each take.

Penélope Cruz as Pelagia dancing at the Feast of St Gerasimos

Of course, one of the seductions of visiting the set was the prospect of meeting the actors. One of them, David Morrissey, I have known for many years, and have always liked him even though he is so upsettingly tall and good-looking. It was a sort of bonus for me to have him in the film, as indeed it was to have John Hurt, whose playing I have long admired, and who, I thought, was probably the perfect choice for the role of Dr Iannis. I was pleased too, by Nicolas Cage, mainly because he very quickly became Captain Corelli for me, even though I had originally envisaged the character as much shorter and altogether different in manner. There was no opportunity to get to know him personally, but then I doubt whether anyone in the world ever gets to know any megastars personally. They are necessarily surrounded by personnel whose job it is to keep them insulated from all the people who would otherwise become a relentless nuisance, which has the incidental effect of simultaneously shielding them from everyone that they actually would like.

Captain Antonio Corelli (Nicolas Cage) starts to compose 'Pelagia's Song'

As a mere writer I have had only a few indications of the harassment that the famous can experience, and the strange way in which fame makes it difficult to relate to anyone in a normal fashion, but it has been enough to persuade me that I would, again, rather be boiled in oil, or indeed go back to being a schoolteacher, than be a megastar like Nick Cage. In the few scenes that I watched, he got it all just right, and I take my hat off to him.

I had originally hoped that Working Title would find a Greek actress to play Pelagia, and this is what they themselves had planned, but they had been disappointed to find that the usual Greek acting style is too florid to be compatible with the naturalistic one demanded by this film. Even the Greeks agreed, though, that Penélope Cruz seemed just right for Pelagia. She is perfectly adorable and enchanting, and I only regret that she too was impossible to get to know, although in her case it was because she was permanently clamped to her mobile phone. She was probably suffering from being surrounded by too many anglophones, and needed to restore her psychic balance by talking Spanish down the telephone line. If Penélope is not a Greek, then she can certainly pass as one, and there is of course the additional consolation of knowing that the film includes at least one Greek actress of enormous stature, the remarkable Irene Papas.

I suppose that the greatest pleasure lay in encountering the boys of La Scala. These young Italians had been hand-picked for their beauty, their charm, and their singing. My girlfriend fell in love with all of them instantaneously, and it was amusing to see how they had become 'La Scala' exactly as it was portrayed

Members of La Scala arrive in the village excited by the news of the fall of Mussolini

in the novel, to the extent of establishing excellent relations with the young Greek girls in the cast, and singing through their repertoire with great enthusiasm at the slightest excuse.

They invited my girlfriend and me to dinner, and gave us a concert. When I said that I felt moved and touched by this, Angeliki, one of the Greek girls, pulled a wry face and observed, 'You wouldn't believe how often they do this.' Never have I been so often hugged and kissed on the cheeks as I was by the boys of La Scala, who seemed extraordinarily grateful to me for having written the book and thereby giving them a chance to have a part in a major movie. I think they were also affected by being able to recreate a particularly tragic episode of Italian history. More than one told me that they had relations who had been lost or harmed by the war, and one of them said, 'I am doing this for my uncle.' Piero, playing the character of Carlo, said that when he first met me he was so choked with feeling that he had to wander away.

I suppose that the greatest disappointment to me has been the reaction of many of the Greeks. The arrival of the film crew in Sami caused an outbreak of venality among those in commerce, and an outbreak of self-importance among local officials. A rumour went around that the film was to be moved to Turkey unless the situation improved, a rumour which was entirely false, since the alternative had always been to film on Corfu.

The Greek press began to print articles calling the film crew an 'occupation force', and accusing the security men of hospitalizing little girls. Journalists tried to get on the set by disguising themselves as members of the cast, and a local woman rented out her rooftop to a TV company so that the filming could be filmed. Two journalists, both British, but one based in Athens, went around telling old left-wingers that I had libelled them in the book, and asking them for their reaction. Naturally, they expressed outrage, and the journalists dutifully reported this outrage as if it constituted a real story. It was nothing more than a pointless bit of clever trouble-making, using a technique which is a tried and trusted one of the tabloids, but which I had not appreciated was also employed by the 'quality' press.

The mayor of Sami ludicrously told one journalist that he would take me to the European Court of Human Rights over the issue, as if I could not do the same to him for trying to inhibit my freedom of expression. By the time I finally met him he had taken a part in the film as an extra, however, and he told me in all seriousness that he wished to invite me to Sami as an official guest. I was told that it was alleged that his majority depended upon a small number of left-wingers, and perhaps this was an explanation for his curious outburst to the journalist concerned, and his apparent hypocrisy afterwards.

The Greek papers naturally picked up the 'story' of my insult to the left-wing wartime resistance, and created a fuss about it even though that aspect of the novel does not feature in the film. I was left dismayed by what apparently counted as 'news' in the papers, and puzzled as to why everybody was digging around desperately for something negative to put into print. No one, as far as I know, ever mentioned that both the film and the book celebrate the extraordinary heroism of the Greeks in resisting the Italian invasion and defeating it, as well as their resilience during the occupation.

A good friend of mine, Minas Tselentis, who runs a café in Fiskardo, likes to tell me that I have ruined his island. He is only half serious, I hope, but it is a thing that worries me none the less. I was very displeased to see that a bar in Aghia Efimia has abandoned its perfectly good Greek name, and renamed itself 'Captain Corelli's', and I dread the idea that sooner or later there might be Captain Corelli Tours, or Pelagia Apartments. I would hate it if Cephallonia were to become as awful as Corfu is in many places, with rashes of vile discotheques, and bad tavernas full of drunken Brits on two-week, swinish binges.

I can only hope that the film does not alter the kind of tourist who goes there. Those who visited because they liked the book were types who wanted to look at memorials, eat the excellent fish, and admire the scenery, and I fear that the film may bring others who are less well-behaved. If so, I sincerely hope that the sensible Cephallonians will put peace above profit, and make sure that the tourist police kick them out without ceremony. As for me, I feel as though I cannot go to Cephallonia any more anyway, partly because I do not now feel entirely comfortable or welcome, and partly because it is a place where I can no longer be anonymous. I know that if my love affair with Greece is to continue, it will have to do so in another place, about which I shall not write a word.

At the time of writing this introduction, the film is in the process of being edited, and I do not know how it is turning out. I am still at the stage of 'fingers crossed'. When it is finished, however, I know that I shall have a sense of closure. If I do not feel that the book has become 'super legitimate', I will at least know that the book has gone to the limit of its trajectory, and that finally I am free to become the author of something else.

Preface
MASSACRE –
THE TRUE STORY

'I dream of the dead. For me they stayed young, as they were back then. For me they are not dead, they remain alive in my memory. They remain alive and young, whilst I am old. They are alive and young everywhere. I may go on living for one, two or fifty years and I will get older and older. They are always young and this is the great beauty of memory. Sometimes I regret that I wasn't killed. It might have been better to have died with them.'

It sounds like a piece of poetry, but it is not. They are the moving words of an old man who survived the massacre on Cephallonia in which thousands upon thousands of unarmed Italian soldiers were murdered by their German captors, after surrendering.

While Louis de Bernières' novel *Captain Corelli's Mandolin* is a work of fiction – a love story, but also a superb evocation of the idiocy of war – the brutal slaughter of the Italians, which is featured so vividly in the novel, is a matter of historical fact. Yet still nearly sixty years since the Second World War ended, this dark episode, even by wartime standards, remains a relatively unknown story, nowhere more so than in Italy itself.

Benito Mussolini, Italy's Fascist leader, took his country into the Second World War on 10 June 1940, when he declared war on Britain and France, hoping that he could share the spoils of Hitler's seemingly unstoppable run of victories, in the shape of territorial gains. His forces' first attack on France that month was curtailed by the French surrender to Germany soon after. In October 1940, keen to prove that he was far from simply being Hitler's lapdog, he turned his attention to British-occupied Egypt, which his forces attacked unsuccessfully from Libya, an Italian colony.

On 28 October 1940, Mussolini gave Greece a humiliating ultimatum, demanding that it allow Italian troops to occupy strategic points within the country. Ithaca-born Greek leader Ioannis Metaxas, expressing the feelings of the nation, rejected the demand without discussion and, even now, 28 October is known as *Ochi* or No Day and remains a public holiday in Greece.

When fiction meets fact. The moment in *Captain Corelli's Mandolin* when the unarmed Italians are gunned down by German forces

Furious at the response, Mussolini launched an attack on Greece through Albania later that day. The assault, with no naval or air support, was conducted mainly by poorly equipped raw conscripts, who lacked even boots. To compound this, the soldiers were fighting in the rainy season, during which temperatures at night often drop below freezing. The Greeks fought back furiously, with help from the British Royal Air Force, which bombed Italian positions. Within three weeks the disastrous Italian attack had been repulsed and Greece now had control of one-third of Albania.

In response to the attack on Greece, Churchill ordered British forces to occupy airfields on Crete and some in Greece. The British military aid to Greece was only token, though, as Metaxas was anxious to avoid provoking German aggression. He died in January 1941 and his successor, Emmanuel Tsouderos, agreed to accept a 53,000-strong British force (half of which were Australians and New Zealanders) as Hitler's expansionary plans for the Balkans became clear.

In addition, Hitler did not want British aircraft to be within striking distance of his primary source of oil, the Ploiesti fields in Romania, and also knew that Crete could be used as a springboard to attack the Balkan coast. He began to prepare an attack against Greece. At 5.30 a.m., on 6 April 1941, twenty-eight Italian divisions and 320 Italian aircraft, including some Italian built and flown Junkers Ju-87 Stuka dive-bombers, in conjunction with huge numbers of German motorized divisions, invaded Yugoslavia and Greece in Operation Marita.

In his order of the day to German troops, Hitler said: 'The fight on Greek soil is not a battle against the Greek people, but against that archenemy, England, which is again trying to extend the war far into the south-east Balkans, the same as he tried far in the north last year. For this reason, on this very spot in the Balkans, we shall fight shoulder to shoulder with our ally until the last Briton has found his Dunkerque in Greece. If any Greeks support this British course, then those Greeks will fall at the same time as the British.'

The Greek army, consisting of 430,000 men, fought valiantly to hold the defensive Metaxas line north-east of Salonika. But by one short thrust to Salonika, the Germans forced the surrender of the line on 9 April. By 22 April, the Greek First Army had surrendered and by 30 April, the British were forced to withdraw from Greece, which they did at a cost of 12,000 men either killed or captured. Greece surrendered on the same day, and a month later Crete fell to a German airborne assault.

On 30 April, Italian paratroops flying on SM-82 aircraft from the southern Italian city of Lecce landed on Cephallonia, spearheading an invasion the following day by the 33rd Acqui Division of the Royal Italian Army commanded by General Antonio Gandin. In the face of overwhelming superiority not a shot was fired against the invaders and within weeks they had fully occupied the island, with a strength of 11,500 men and 525 officers.

By June 1941, Greece was under a tripartite German, Italian, and Bulgarian occupation. King George II and his government-in-exile fled to the Middle East. Over the coming months on Cephallonia, although food was short, there was an air of phoney war. However, for relatives of the men who had been conscripted into the Greek army and had been killed during the Italian and German mainland invasion, the reality was all too painful and many of those who had survived were living harsh lives as partisans.

On mainland Greece the situation was more acute. The invading forces requisitioned food stocks over the winter of 1941 to 1942 and around 100,000 starved. Of Greece's 76,000-strong Jewish population, 46,000 were sent to Auschwitz, with only a few surviving, although some Italian commanders, mainly in Corfu and the north, were unwilling to put German anti-Jewish measures into effect.

Louis de Bernières' novel *Captain Corelli's Mandolin* paints a picture of invaders and the subjugated living in relative harmony, and this does appear to be the case on Cephallonia. The conscripts of the Italian army did not seem to support Mussolini's expansionism. For most, their aim was simply to bide their time until they could return to their families. For the Cephallonians, though,

The Italians arrive on Cephallonia in *Captain Corelli's Mandolin*. Their overwhelming numbers mean they are unopposed

life was far from idyllic; food was short and medical supplies almost non-existent. There were outbreaks of malaria, although there is some anecdotal evidence that the Italians gave quinine to the Greeks. Compared to those living under a German regime, the Cephallonians' lives were considerably more tolerable, but lack of medicine meant that illness was more common.

Kate Iakovatou-Tool, whose family ran a distillery and winery in Argostoli, kept a diary during the war. Her entry for Tuesday, 26 January 1943, reveals just how difficult conditions became:

> *An epidemic hit the village of Damouliata five days ago. Meningitis was diagnosed following blood tests and the removal of liquid from the spine. Five children have already died.*

Interestingly, on Friday, 30 April 1943, her diary also makes reference to radical leaflets distributed to Italian soldiers on the island, which in de Bernières' novel were written by Iannis and Carlo and printed by Kokolios:

Penélope Cruz as Pelagia. Life for the people of Cephallonia during the wartime occupation was tough

> *Proclamations were found yesterday in Argostoli urging the army to mutiny. A search was conducted in Argostoli but people say it was written by Italians.*

Former Acqui Division captain Amos Pampaloni was in his thirties when he was posted to Cephallonia. He recalls: 'For Italians, all Greeks were like brothers. If an Italian soldier had a piece of bread, he would cut it and give it to a man or a woman. For us, going to Corfu or Cephallonia was like going on a holiday. From my camp, I would go to Argostoli on my horse each night. I had become friends with the best families in Argostoli. I was friends with the director of the post office, the pharmacist and a lawyer. They invited me to dinner every night and I ate at their houses. Lots of Italians fell in love with many Greek women and many Greek women were in love with Italians.'

Pampaloni's story has some interesting parallels with that of de Bernières' fictional character Antonio Corelli although, as the author says, he 'didn't know enough about Appollonio [Renzo Appollonio was one of Pampaloni's lieutenants, whereas in de Bernières' novel it is a Captain Fienzo Appollonio who opens fire on the Germans first] and Pampaloni at the time of writing to use them as a source of character'.

Pampaloni was conscripted to fight for his country in 1940 and sent to Cephallonia in 1941. He fell in love with a local girl who he would meet every

Captain Corelli and
Dr Iannis at the Italian
encampment

evening; his sweetheart was a schoolteacher's daughter called Maria. He was involved in the battle with the Germans and survived the German firing-squad machine guns. Although wounded, he was left for dead under bodies. His wounds were treated by a village doctor and after recovery he joined the ELAS Greek partisans.

The relatively quiet time for troops on Cephallonia between 1941 and 1943 was not matched by that faced by the Italians' brothers-in-arms elsewhere. Poor command and low morale, combined with conscripts unwilling to fight so far from home, gave rise to Italy losing its large empire in Africa including Ethiopia by early 1941, and 250,000 troops were sent to bolster the German army in Russia. Meanwhile, at home, civilian morale was low (partially due to bombing), food was short, and by 1943 Mussolini commanded neither respect nor obedience.

The final straw came with the Allies' landing on Sicily in July 1943, which soon came under their control. Between 24 and 25 July, the Fascist Grand Council met in Rome for the first time since the beginning of the war. It passed a motion asking King Victor Emmanuel III to resume his full constitutional powers and to sack Mussolini, which he did the same day, installing Marshal Pietro Badoglio as prime minister. Mussolini was arrested but later rescued by the Germans. After setting up a republic in northern Italy, in 1945 he tried to escape to Switzerland but was captured by Italian partisans and shot near Lake Como. His body was then brought back for public display in Milan.

On 3 September 1943, Marshal Pietro Badoglio, prime minister and head of the Italian government forces, secretly signed an armistice and surrender with General Dwight Eisenhower, Commander in Chief of the Allied forces. It was a further five days, though, before the surrender was announced on Rome Radio. Badoglio said:

'The Italian Government, recognizing the impossibility of continuing the unequal struggle against the overwhelming power of the enemy, with the object of avoiding further and more grievous harm to the nation, has requested an armistice from General Eisenhower, Commander in Chief of the Anglo-American Allied forces. This request has been granted. The Italian forces will therefore cease all acts of hostility against the Anglo-American forces wherever they may be met. They will, however, oppose attack from any other quarter.'

The same day General Eisenhower made the following proclamation on United Nations Radio:

'This is General Dwight D. Eisenhower, Commander in Chief of the Allied forces. The Italian Government has surrendered its armed forces unconditionally. As Allied Commander in Chief, I have granted a military armistice, the terms of which have been approved by the governments of the United Kingdom, the United States and the Union of Soviet Socialist Republics. Thus I am acting in the interest of the United Nations.

Members of La Scala during happier times, enjoying time off on the beach

'Hostilities between the armed forces of the United Nations and those of Italy terminate at once. All Italians who now act to help eject the German aggressor from Italian soil will have the assistance and the support of the United Nations.'

The timing of the announcement of the Italian capitulation was a surprise, but it was a move Hitler and his forces had anticipated. A month before 1,800 troops of the German 966th Grenadier Regiment, under the command of Lieutenant-Colonel Hans Barge, had arrived on Cephallonia. The immediate reaction of the German High Command in Berlin to Italy's surrender was to put Operation Konstantin into effect. It allowed for the immediate seizure of control of all Italian-occupied areas and the disarming of any Italian forces that refused to continue to fight alongside Germany.

On Cephallonia there was confusion and indecision at the highest level in the Italian ranks, although most soldiers thought the surrender to the Allies would mean they would soon be home with their families. General Gandin, however, received no orders or even guidance from the now practically dissolved Italian command. He sought direction from senior General Carlo Vecchiarelli in Athens, who replied: 'Italian troops are not to take armed initiative against the Germans; they are not to fraternize with Anglo-Americans or local partisans; everyone is to remain at his place, maintaining exemplary discipline.'

Captain Corelli and his men are faced with a demand from the Germans to give up their weapons

The statement was compatible with Badoglio's announcement that Italian armed forces would 'oppose attack from any other quarter', but in Gandin's mind and that of his men was also Eisenhower's statement to them that: 'All Italians who now act to help eject the German aggressor from Italian soil will have the assistance and the support of the United Nations.' At the same time as this, Lieutenant-Colonel Barge demanded that the Italians surrender and hand over their weapons and called in reinforcements.

The mood among the rank-and-file Italian men and some officers was resistant to the demand to surrender to the Germans. They were, after all, an undefeated force and considerably stronger in numbers than the Germans. In addition, they believed that the Allies would come to their aid if they resisted the Germans, and rumours were abounding about the fate of the Italian forces on Corfu who were thought to have surrendered. Above all, as Acqui Division veteran Giovanni Pampaloni (no relation) says: 'They were soldiers who had served in the army for three to four years without leave and they wanted to return to their houses. They despaired at the thought of becoming prisoners, of not being able to return to home for who knows how long.'

In Argostoli, there was a growing feeling that relations between the Italian and the Germans were about to reach a crucial point. As Kate Iakovatou-Tool recorded in her diary entry for Friday, 10 September:

Worrying news about the position taken by the Germans and Italians. The Germans hauled down the Italian flag at night, but a young Italian officer pulled up another one.

The following day she wrote:

The climate of nervousness continues unabated. The rumours are that an Italian ship tried to depart but returned after receiving fire from the Germans. When it was dark, a (requisitioned) caique took about 300 Germans to Argostoli. They demanded to take over the Municipality from the Italians, who refused and fortified it. Great fears of an outbreak of war and we hear that the Italians have given arms to some of our men as well.

Armando Crivelaro who, at age nineteen, arrived in Cephallonia in June 1943 as part of reinforcements and was stationed at St Gerasimos, explains the feeling of the ordinary soldier. 'The Germans wanted to disarm us but we didn't want to give them our weapons,' he says. 'We only wanted to surrender our arms once we had gone to Italy and we actually revolted against our superiors.'

At the time, Crivelaro had no idea of the extreme measures that the Germans would resort to if he and his comrades surrendered. They simply expected to be taken prisoner. 'If we had given up our arms [we thought] we would have been taken prisoner to Germany like the 3,000 who were sunk in the ship [the *Ardenna*].'

Finally, it is claimed, a referendum was organized, some say by General Gandin, asking whether the men should hand over their weapons and surrender or resist the Germans. There was a resounding vote in favour of fighting their former allies. Early on 13 September 1943, the Italian forces began their offensive when an artillery battery fired on two German barges, sinking one and capturing a second.

Kate Iakovatou-Tool's diary for that day states:

Captain Corelli leads from the front as he and his countrymen attempt to resist the German invasion

The sound of explosions and machine guns woke us up at 06.00 in the morning. It sounded as if fighting was taking place in Argostoli. Widespread panic. Most fled to the plains, including the priest's family. I stayed at home with Angeliki despite pleas to the contrary. The machine and field gun fire continued till about 13.30. I peacefully drank my coffee and cooked, having faith in God and St Haralambos.

The following day troops of the élite German 1st Alpine Division arrived on the island. As Armando Crivelaro recalls: 'We fought the Germans and in the beginning pushed them back towards the sea. Then German reinforcements arrived from Lixouri and from the north. Then they came down from the mountains towards us below in the valley.'

On 15 September, German Stuka dive-bombers began to hammer Italian positions dropping their deadly cargo of either a 1,100-pound or a 550-pound and two 110-pound bombs. With few anti-aircraft guns and no air cover, despite the fact that there were Italian, British and American aircraft within range of the island, the Italians' strength in numbers was little match for the combined might of the German forces. Nevertheless for the next six days, despite intensive bombing, the Italians fought valiantly, in one case continuing to fire on advancing German troops from olive trees that caught fire.

A German Stuka. Lack of anti-aircraft guns and air cover was the key factor which turned the tide of battle against the Italians

'We were all against the Germans,' one veteran says. 'We were convinced that all the other Italians had more or less done the same thing. We were calm and in the first days of combat the Germans lost a lot of territory. If we had fought for two days more without the aeroplanes the entire island would have come into Italian hands. The German aeroplanes won the war, not the German troops.'

Amos Pampaloni recalls: 'We fought from dawn to sunset with aeroplanes bombing us.'

Despite the Italians' larger number of troops, it was their total lack of any air support, and the Luftwaffe's consequent mastery of the skies with the ability to target all the Italian forces freely, that made it an unequal fight. As they dived for an attack, the Stukas' familiar fierce scream (from cardboard sirens fitted to both the aircraft and its bombs by engineers, deliberately to cause maximum psychological damage to enemy confidence) would have only helped to sap the morale of the Italian troops.

Amos Pampaloni continues, 'The conditions were such that we were forced to remain hidden and immobile. We were in a very difficult position.'

Giovanni Pampaloni says that the absence of air support meant 'it was a battle lost from the start', adding that 'one of our battalions lost two-thirds of their men in one hour. It was terrible because they could do nothing but be hit.'

As they fought, the Italians expected Allied forces to arrive in their support any day, and, at the very least, give some air support. Yet no one came to their aid. As one Italian soldier says: 'Day by day we were expecting to see an English, American or even an Italian aeroplane but nothing came.'

The matter of whether Greek partisans fought alongside the Italians against the Germans remains controversial. Even first-hand accounts seem to differ. Armando Crivelaro states that: 'We opened our supplies depot and they took knives and bombs for the fight against the Germans. In the end they were killed, too. In Havriata the Germans filled thirty-six cisterns [underground reservoirs for rainwater] with the dead. Twenty-five years later a Greek told me that they found bones of Italians and Greeks together there.' According to Amos Pampaloni, though, the partisans 'helped us but they didn't fight with us'.

Realizing that their position was hopeless – and having lost 1,300 men in just nine days – on 22 September General Gandin ordered his men to lay down their arms. Weary from battle and dejected by defeat, the Italians were disarmed by their enemies. Ordinary soldiers were then separated from their officers and most men then believed they would be sent home or to German prisoner-of-war camps.

Instead, over the next few days, in twenty-three sites – olive groves, fields, near buildings and by the sea – the Germans began systematically slaughtering 5,200 of their estimated 10,000 unarmed prisoners, on the direct order of Adolf Hitler himself who was furious that the Italians had dared to attack his forces.

Defeated and dejected: Italian soldiers after surrendering

CAPTAIN CORELLI'S MANDOLIN

Some bodies were
hidden in underground
reservoirs, others were
simply left in the open

There is considerable anecdotal evidence that the Germans tricked their prisoners into thinking they were going to be sent home. It clearly did not occur to the Italians that their former allies would react in such a violent manner. Keeping their plans secret, however, enabled the Germans in almost all cases to use just a few men to kill hundreds of Italians. In Farsa, for example, just eleven German soldiers were responsible for the execution of 200 Italians.

One Cephallonian, who was six at the time, recalls playing with friends in the middle of a field at Procopata and then being ordered by German soldiers to leave. 'There was a stone wall behind the field and we sat on the wall and watched,' says Lakis. 'The Germans offered the Italians cigarettes and someone gave them food. It seemed like the Italians were happy and the Germans were telling them: "Italia, Italia!", indicating that they would send them to Italy.

'We heard the Italians laughing and shouting "Italia, Italia" and they seemed to be happy. The Germans put the Italians into a line. I don't think they probably suspected anything. But the Germans had placed four machine guns at the edge of the field.'

None of the Germans noticed the children as, without warning, they opened fire, wiping out the Italians in a few seconds. Afterwards the Germans rounded up a few local men, including Lakis's father, and forced them to stack the bodies in piles. According to Lakis, some bodies were also thrown into a nearby well until it was full. About an hour after the shooting more Germans arrived with petrol and set the piles of bodies alight. 'They burned all of them,' he recalls. 'We watched them and they were burning for a whole day. The bodies appeared to be moving with the flames.'

Lakis's testimony also supports the theory that some Italians, although grievously and probably fatally wounded, were not yet dead at the point – although what he witnessed, of course, could equally be the tightening of a corpse's skin in the heat.

After the shooting, one wounded Italian waited until the Germans had left and then separated himself from his dead compatriots. 'He dragged his body to the stone wall and fell into a ditch behind,' Lakis remembers. 'It turned out to be Othelo, a soldier who had previously given us food when we had been hungry. My sister found him in the ditch. Then she and a friend helped him and took him to a hut 500 yards away.'

The soldier was one of just two survivors of that particular shooting. Elsewhere, many others who were not killed in the initial gunfire were tricked into revealing that they were still alive and then killed. 'When the Germans said: "Enough, we have finished with the shooting", sixteen survivors came forth and were shot on the spot,' recalls one survivor.

Only two survived because they were buried beneath the corpses. Louisa Caleffi, whose late husband Guido was among the survivors, says: 'Some of them hadn't died. The Germans said: "Whoever isn't dead, let him get up and we will grant him his life." No one moved because anyone who did was shot at.'

Following orders: Captain Günter Weber (David Morrissey) surrounded by the bodies of the La Scala men

Armando Crivelaro recalls: 'They executed between 300 and 600 of us. I survived beneath the corpses.' Afterwards he was found by Greek partisans. He later joined them, but then, after falling ill, managed to get back to Italy by boat.

None of the Italians could have anticipated the German reaction. Amos Pampaloni says: 'We thought we were going to fight against honest soldiers, not criminals and scoundrels who took prisoners and executed them,' he says. 'We never expected this, we never thought that they would execute prisoners.'

Pampaloni and eighty of his countrymen were cornered by German forces in the village of Dilinata on 22 September: 'After the soldiers had disarmed us, they began taking off our watches, chains, wallets and belts,' he told *The Guardian* newspaper. 'I protested to the captain in charge that it was not permitted to take prisoners' personal effects. He replied through an interpreter: "Not from prisoners, but from traitors, yes." They told us to stand in a row and I was made to go at the end of the line, Lieutenant Tognato next to me. He called out to the soldiers to say their prayers, but I had no idea what was about to happen and told him not to demoralize the men.

'The captain said: "Let's go." I took a step, he raised his pistol and fired a single shot at me. The bullet went through my neck and I was thrown to the ground by the impact. That must have been the signal for the massacre, because they then opened up with machine guns and I could hear the cries of our boys calling "mamma" and "Dio". I never lost consciousness and felt one of the Germans take off my watch, which they had missed earlier because it was on my right hand. After about ten minutes I heard the Germans march off, laughing and singing.'

The awful truth: the moment Corelli and Carlo (Piero Maggio) realize exactly what the Germans plan to do with them and their compatriots

(Above) General Antonio Gandin, the Italian commander on Cephallonia, was among those to die. (Opposite, above) Major Harald von Hirschfeld, who was promoted after the massacre

Partially covered by Tognato's body, Pampaloni lay still, bleeding from his wounds. Later he was found by a Greek boy who brought him water.

Many officers, said to be around 180, were treated differently from their men, but faced the same eventual fate. They were rounded up and taken to a building, known as The Red House at San Teodoro near Argostoli. 'The trucks arrived slowly and German soldiers jumped on to a few officers like crows, grabbing them by their wrists to take their watches,' recalls a survivor. 'They searched their pockets and their wallets and pulled off their wedding rings.'

As they approached death, the men's faith remained strong. 'Many of the men lifted their arms to the sky, while others were holding prayer books,' says the eyewitness. 'Some stared at an icon or medallion that they took off their necks. Many took photographs of their loved one from their pockets and showed them to the soldier close to them. Many confessed, whilst others wrote personal notes to their loved ones far away. They gave the notes to military priest Don Formato. Some German soldiers guarding us seemed to be sad, other seemed indifferent and some looked at us smiling, saying: "Kaput, kaput!"'

By all accounts the men faced impending death stoically, such as the captain who told a priest just before he was shot: 'Father, father, I have five sons and one on the way.' 'Tell my children how their father was killed,' said another witness. Then he presented himself for execution with his pipe in his mouth.

Then men were called for execution in groups of eight. 'Always more than eight presented themselves,' says the witness, 'but they were kicked away. If you must die, it is best to confront death immediately rather than to die with anxiety.'

Many of the bodies were thrown over the cliff into the sea, some weighted so that they would sink, others not. The body of General Gandin, who, it is claimed, was among the first to be killed, was never found. Eventually Don Formato, the Italian military chaplain, to whom the last notes and belongings of the massacred men had been given, met the same fate as his compatriots, the Germans showing no respect for his office. Afterwards the surviving members of the Acqui Division were sent to Germany. One ship, the *Ardenna*, is believed to have hit a mine, though some reports suggest that it was deliberately sunk by the Germans. All 3,000 men aboard were lost. It was a tragic irony that, after surviving a terrible massacre, they should be drowned at sea.

The massacre on Cephallonia was not an isolated incident. On Corfu more than 600 Italians were murdered and in Santi Quaranta in Albania, 120 Italian officers with the Perugia Division were killed, but the fate of its commander, General Ernesto Chiminello, was particularly horrific. In October 1943, while attempting to arrange surrender with German forces, he was captured. His throat was cut and then he was decapitated and his head was placed on top of a flagpole as a macabre warning to the Albanian population.

The Germans evacuated Cephallonia in September 1944. After the war General Hubert Lanz, Commander of XXII Mountain Army Corps, one of the

(Opposite, below) In the film, the killing of some of their countrymen in cold blood helped convince the Italians to resist the German demand to surrender

two men on the ground responsible for implementing the massacre (the other, Major Harald von Hirschfeld had been promoted to General after the massacre but was subsequently killed in Warsaw, Poland in 1945) was put on trial at the International Military Tribunal War Crimes Court at Nuremberg in 1947, where he was sentenced to twelve years' imprisonment.

Now there is little physical reminder of the appalling events of that week in September 1943, except for the memories of a few now elderly local people who recall the young Italians, laughing, joking in the months before the battle and then how they were cut down in a few seconds of gunfire.

In 1978 a memorial to the men of the Acqui Division was installed overlooking Argostoli. On either side of a white cross are lists of the site of the battles and of the massacres. In the bright sunshine of modern-day Cephallonia – a perfect place for a holiday – it is almost impossible to believe that such carnage ever took place. After all, it looks like paradise, but the reality in 1943 – as so poignantly brought to life now in the film of *Captain Corelli's Mandolin* – was hell.

Chapter 1
BESTSELLER TO SCREENPLAY

It is 1941 and Captain Antonio Corelli, a young Italian officer,
is posted to the Greek island of Cephallonia as part of the
occupying forces. At first he is ostracized by the locals, but as a
conscientious but far from fanatical soldier, whose main aim is to
have a peaceful war, he proves in time to be civilized, humorous –
and a consummate musician.
When the local doctor's daughter's letters to her fiancé – and
members of the underground – go unanswered, the working of the
eternal triangle seems inevitable. But can this fragile love survive
as a war of bestial savagery gets closer and the lines are drawn
between invader and defender?

Louis de Bernières' stunning novel *Captain Corelli's Mandolin*, which explores turbulent times on the tiny Greek island of Cephallonia during the years of Italian occupation, has now sold almost two million copies and been translated into twenty languages. It has won international writing awards and reaped plaudits from around the world. An astonishing achievement, the novel has moved, excited, entertained and entranced its readers in an extraordinary but, at the same time, ordinary world of rich, colourful yet real characters, and breathtakingly beautiful locations, set against a backdrop of a world in turmoil.

As distinguished writer A.S. Byatt said of *Captain Corelli's Mandolin*: 'Gleeful comedy and true terror make a peculiarly English fictive mixture, and Louis de Bernières is in the direct line that runs through Dickens and Evelyn Waugh . . . he has only to look into the world, one senses, for it to rush into reality, colours and touch and taste.'

Now, thanks to director John Madden's $45 million Hollywood film adaptation of the novel, millions more will be introduced to – and captivated by – the richness and humanity of the world of *Captain Corelli's Mandolin*.

While – as is nearly always the case when a book is adapted from book to film – some significant changes have been made to the plot of the novel, the

Pelagia at the
Ag Fanentes
Monastery

The love story between Corelli and Pelagia is the centrepiece of the film

film script has succeeded in remaining faithful to the spirit and depth of the original; avoided introducing too much Hollywood gloss and managed to recreate the world depicted so vividly by Louis de Bernières.

The central core of the film reflects that of the novel – a powerful romance set in the midst of a war that, having brought death and destruction to much of the world, finally comes to the magical Greek island of Cephallonia with horrendous consequences for civilians and soldiers alike. 'It's an epic romance in the same genre as *Doctor Zhivago* and *The English Patient*,' says Tim Bevan, one of the film's producers. 'It's about life and death and is full of raw emotion. It's set on a big canvas, with big emotions, big characters, and very beautiful scenery. With this film we are going to take the audience on a journey to a place they never thought they'd go to, to meet people they never thought they'd meet, to learn about something based on fact that they never thought they'd learn . . . If, at the end of the day, we achieve that, we'll have the perfect movie.'

It was autumn 1994 when producer Kevin Loader bought a hardback copy of *Captain Corelli's Mandolin* and, while reading it, was immediately struck by the possibility of making it into a film. With its period setting and the necessity to shoot much, if not all of it on location – probably in Greece – it was clear to Loader that it would be an expensive film to make and would therefore need to be made for the cinema rather than for television.

Excited by the idea, he bought a second copy of the book and gave it to his friend and colleague, director Roger Michell. 'I told him I thought there was a fantastic movie in it,' recalls Loader, a tall, amiable man whose looks and cheerful disposition give him a youthful air. 'Roger then sat on it for months – literally months. And, by the time he finally read it, which was in the spring of 1995, the paperback version had come out and was just starting to create a bit of a buzz. Roger loved it – could see its potential as a film – but said the story would need severe pruning and a lot of editing.'

Loader made enquiries about whether the film rights were still available. They were, but in the few months since he had read the book, other production companies had been struck by de Bernières' work, and had also made enquiries.

Loader describes what took place next as 'a kind of beauty contest'. He explains: 'We all took Louis out for lunch and outlined our visions.'

He cannot recall exactly what was said during their lunch, but clearly he and Roger Michell must have impressed de Bernières, because, as Loader ventured, 'The choice Louis made at that point was probably based not so much on what we said but on who we were.'

Loader, who began his career as a BBC drama producer, first worked with Michell in 1992 when he hired him to direct Hanif Kureishi's *Buddha of Suburbia*. He and Michell became friends and went on to collaborate on British television's production of the successful stage play *My Night With Reg*, by Kevin Elyot, and the documentary about the Indian actor Harish Patel, *Ready When You Are Mr Patel*. 'The fact that we had worked on literary material before for television probably meant that de Bernières saw us as a safe duo,' says Loader.

Having, then, been chosen as the author's preferred candidates to make the book into a film, Loader and Michell needed to face up to the financial reality of their selection. The novel, which was by now selling in huge quantities, was increasingly being noted by other film-makers and the cost, therefore, of buying the option to turn it into a film was also rising.

'Sebastian Born, who was managing the screen deal for Louis, was frank,' Loader recalls. 'He said: "I'm looking for quite a lot of money for this."'

In general, options – the amount of money paid to writers for the rights for a fixed period of time to translate their work on to the big or small screen – can be bought relatively cheaply in the United Kingdom, especially when compared to rights purchased in the United States.

Pelagia in the village after the German invasion

Before the turmoil of war comes to Cephallonia Mandras (Christian Bale) and Pelagia look to the future together

'So we knew at that point that it was going to be an expensive book to option in addition to an expensive film to make. At that stage, though, I don't think we even imagined we would get a Hollywood star of Nick Cage's stature because we still thought it was going to be a $25 million movie.

'To be frank – and I think this shows how much British film-making has changed in the last five years – there was hardly anybody we could go to in the UK who could realistically finance a $25 million movie. We only had two places to try – Miramax or Working Title.'

The alternative for Loader and Michell was the United States, but neither was keen to seek finance there.

'Friends in Hollywood faxed me the Hollywood agencies' and studios' coverage of the book,' Loader recalls. 'But these suggested to me they didn't really understand the book. They just didn't think it was commercial – didn't see beyond de Bernières' rather discursive style to what is at the core of the novel – a fantastically moving love story with different, quirky, interesting characters set against a very, very traumatic but completely absorbing piece of history.

'They just didn't get that and, instead, were put off by large sections of the novel concerning Mussolini, a cat and chapters called *L'Omosessuale*. From the point of view of Hollywood script readers, you can see the book looked like a pretty tall order. So at that time Roger and I decided not to go to Hollywood because we thought they would probably pull out their readers' reports and say: "Yeah, we'd love to work with you guys, but we don't want to do this."

'This left us with Miramax or Working Title. Miramax had always been very encouraging but the downside, at that time, was that we didn't know how much freedom we would retain on the project. So we went to Working Title, which was then – and is again now – a European company. It felt like the right place to go because *Captain Corelli's Mandolin* is a European film – and an ambitious European film – and that, essentially, is what Working Title is always interested in making.'

Loader and Michell arranged a meeting with Tim Bevan who, with his partner Eric Fellner, runs Working Title Films. This company, which is owned by Universal Pictures, which in turn is owned by the French company Vivendi Universal, occupies an almost unique position in the film world – and enjoys a considerable measure of autonomy. From their office in London's Oxford Street, Bevan and Fellner are able to give the green light to five films a year, up to a cost of $25 million each, and fund other small-budget feature films through their new WT2 label.

Their track record for producing hit movies is impressive. In the seven years from 1992, when Fellner joined the company, until 1999, Working Title made fifteen films at a cost of $193 million with gross revenues of nearly $1 billion. Those successes included *Four Weddings and a Funeral, Bean, Elizabeth, Notting Hill, Fargo* and *Billy Elliot.*

Loader recalls: 'We took *Captain Corelli* to Tim on a Friday, and said: "We've won the rights to set it up, think it's going to be quite expensive to develop and make, so don't come into it unless you are serious – and can you let us know on Monday?"'

He did. 'He rang and said: "Yeah, we'll do it – let's talk about writers."'

φ φ φ φ φ

As is the case with most film scripts adapted from novels, Louis de Bernières had no wish to adapt his own work for the big screen. As Loader explained, most novelists – even ones like William Boyd who know how to write a screenplay – don't want to because, in effect, it feels like going back over old ground and rewriting the novel.

Captain Corelli arrives at the doctor's house for the first time and becomes reacquainted with the girl he and his men spotted when they arrived in Argostoli

'At our meeting with Louis,' he explained, 'we did explore the possibility of him writing the screenplay, but he was adamant that he didn't want anything to do with it. This was partly modesty because he had never attempted to write a screenplay and didn't think he could do it – but also a recognition that the process of adapting this kind of book requires the cutting of a huge amount of material. Indeed, our pitch to him was that it was going to involve finding a highway through the novel. Basically, we said we'd concentrate on what happened on the island of Cephallonia, but that all the other fantastical stuff round the edges – because he goes off everywhere in the novel – would be impossible to include.

'He wasn't remotely precious about it. In fact, he was pretty fantastic. He said: "Look, I trust you guys to give it a good go. I'll happily read any drafts of the script you want me to read – you know, let's stay in touch." Which is what we did as the drafts progressed over the next four or five years.'

In selling the film rights of his book, had de Bernières relinquished control over his work?

'I don't think you'd ever give a novelist veto over a film,' says Loader. 'That would be an insane thing to do. Generally film companies take a very hard line over that. The writer Nick Hornby summed this up well in an article about his novel *High Fidelity* which was subsequently turned into a film. He said the

Iannis and Father Arsenios (Dimitris Kamperidis) breakfast at the *kapheneion*

thing about selling the film rights of your book is that it's like selling anything else. Once you've sold it, it belongs to someone else and you have to be quite grown-up about that.'

The first name in the frame to write the film script for *Captain Corelli's Mandolin* was South African-born Shawn Slovo – daughter of Ruth First, the murdered anti-apartheid activist, and Joe Slovo, former communist and ANC leader – whose account of her childhood was turned into the successful film *A World Apart*.

'Shawn had been working with Working Title for several years and Roger and I had read quite a lot of her scripts,' Loader recalls. 'We all agreed she was one of the best screenwriters in England. She had a very solid background in script- and story-editing and was very strong on screen narrative.'

At that early stage important decisions had to be made concerning the transformation of the story from book to screen. Essentially, this involved deciding what material should be cut for the film version and making decisions about languages and accents. Loader and Michell had their own views, but it was vital they and Slovo should agree before she began her first draft.

Lemoni (Joanna-Daria Adraktas) plays in the olive groves

'We'd obviously thought conceptually about how we would deal with the accent and culture problems,' says Loader, 'because the novel involves people of three nationalities, none of whom is English or American. Obviously we had to think about how we were going to deal with the language issue from an early stage.

'The bottom line was that in order to get the amount of money we needed to make the film, we had to make it in English. So we made the decision that it would *all* be in English and would *all* be in accented English . . . But that obviously created certain restraints when we started to think about casting. There are some disastrous precedents when you start to mix nationalities. If, for example, you watch a movie such as *Roseanna's Grave*, which is all set in a small Italian village, it has Jean Reno playing an Italian with a French accent speaking English! *Roseanna's Grave* is a very good script, but the film was completely sunk by the problem with accents.'

According to Loader, however, Steven Spielberg's epic *Schindler's List* found the perfect solution.

'*Schindler* is the film that faces up to this problem most perfectly,' he says. 'So we tried to analyse what it was about this film that worked so effortlessly and so convincingly. I think there are two things: first, they mixed the original languages up with the English very well indeed. So in a scene where Jewish

prisoners are having a medical to assess who should go to the labour camps and who shouldn't, everything would be going on in German when suddenly Ralph Fiennes, as German army officer Amon Goeth, comes banging into the scene with a German accent but speaking in English, and the transition is fantastically smooth. They would then put a bit of the original languages – German, Yiddish and Polish – round the edge of the frame.

'The other thing was that there were no American actors in the film. Spielberg cast either Polish actors or English actors with accents. I don't know why it is, but it is easier for English audiences to accept English actors with other nationalities' accents than American actors with accents. I also think lots of American actors find it technically difficulty to lose the American in their voice.

'So, the one thing that was blindingly obvious to us at that stage of making *Captain Corelli's Mandolin* was that if we had too heavy a hint of American in the middle of this movie then we would sink it just as easily as if we had a Frenchman playing Corelli. Later on that would lead us in certain directions when casting but, at the beginning, in scripting terms, we just needed to agree to write it in English.'

Shooting was scheduled for the summer of 1999, although at a very early stage the possibility of filming as early as the summer of 1998 was discussed. Working Title, however, was keen for Roger Michell to direct another of its films first, Richard Curtis's *Notting Hill*, starring Julia Roberts and Hugh Grant. Then, if *Notting Hill* proved to be a success – which it was (it took more than $115 million at the American box office alone) – it would be a further boost to Michell's reputation and help to increase the box-office prospects for *Captain Corelli's Mandolin*.

By Christmas 1998 it was becoming apparent that editing on *Notting Hill* was likely to run into the spring of 1999, and that plans to shoot *Captain Corelli's Mandolin* in the summer of 1999 would need to be revised. 'Roger was supposed to be clear of *Notting Hill* by Christmas 1998,' Loader says, 'but he was still in the cutting-room tinkering with it in March 1999. Frustratingly, it meant we missed the '99 window.'

The positive side of the delay meant that there would be more time for casting. The first serious discussion about this came in the spring of 1999, when it was agreed that the part of Corelli would have to be played by a box-office draw – probably an American star but possibly a British one.

'By this time,' Loader says, 'Julia Roberts was going all over Hollywood saying Roger was the greatest director she'd ever worked with. And once *Notting Hill* opened – and did really well – Roger suddenly became a director with real clout, and life got easier on the casting front. From then on, we felt we could ask for any actor and be given a serious hearing.'

Those words soon proved to be true. The potential for the plot of *Captain Corelli's Mandolin* to be a great cinematic success was already there; now, in casting terms, there were no restrictions on how ambitious the film could be.

Corelli, Iannis and Pelagia dine on the terrace at the doctor's house

Chapter 2
FINDING CAPTAIN CORELLI

'As an actor, Nick Cage has a wonderful sense of dignity – a kind of honour – which is crucial to Corelli because that is what Pelagia found so attractive and irresistible about him. Nick is also extraordinarily generous and supportive with other actors, and there was a fantastic chemistry and rapport between him and Penélope. So it was a wholly enjoyable experience. Even though he is Italian by blood, he'd never been to Italy nor had to act Italian in quite that way, but he mastered a wonderfully consistent Italian accent very quickly. The fact that he also learned to play the mandolin is typical – absolutely typical of his imagination and application.'

John Madden, Director

The list of actors that Roger Michell and Kevin Loader thought might be right for the role of Captain Antonio Corelli was, in Loader's words, 'pretty short'. He explains: 'The role is a difficult part to play because the qualities of the character are not necessarily qualities that modern actors have. Young American actors, in particular, and increasingly the younger generation of British actors, are all really good at cool acting – the "Are you talking to me?" stuff – and have good reactive presences, but they're not very front-footed, not out there, not self-projecting. They're moody, but don't have the walking-on-a-tightrope qualities we needed for Corelli. For him, we needed an actor with soulful energy – and a projective personality. And when we started to compile a list of who this might be, it was pretty short. The actor also had to be able to do a convincing Italian accent without a hint of American – and be able to look convincingly Italian.'

Lots of suggestions were put forward, including two extremely bankable young American stars: Leonardo diCaprio and Matt Damon, along with a slightly older one, Tom Cruise.

Nicolas Cage was considered perfect for the role of Captain Antonio Corelli

'Some Hollywood executives,' Loader says candidly, 'make suggestions based on the list of the top ten stars that week – appropriateness doesn't always seem to matter.'

Nicolas Cage's name, along with that of Johnny Depp and Daniel Day-Lewis, was on the list for Captain Corelli from day one.

'Nick is a very, very good actor,' says Loader. 'Just think of the range of work he has done. There aren't many people who can play an action hero, such as Cameron Poe in *Con Air* and a romantic comedy lead, such as Charlie Lans in *It Could Happen to You*, and can also play the dark dangerous stuff that he has done with Mike Figgis and Martin Scorsese in *Leaving Las Vegas* and *Bringing Out the Dead*. Very few people succeed in that range of parts, which is, of course, why Nick is so much in demand. It's because he is able to go from a Scorsese movie, to a John Woo movie, to our movie.

'Nick was the only person on the list who I really thought: "Wow – of course!" But then the issue was: "Can he be a non-American?" – which was the main concern with all the American possibilities. Obviously there could have been a version of the film where everybody was able to play their own nationality, but that wouldn't have got us the kind of budget we needed to make our film because the facts of life are that for an American audience in particular, an American or British star is a prerequisite.'

Working Title's Tim Bevan agrees: 'One thing I decided right from the start was that I didn't want to make a quaint $10-million "Mediterraneo" version of this film,' he says. 'I felt if we were going to give the film a chance, then we needed to paint the backdrop in fairly vivid detail and find the resources to enable the director to be able to do the battle scenes properly.

'One of the joys for people coming to see this film is being sucked into this rather mysterious place that they never thought they would go to, and if you don't render it properly by doing a film of scale then the audience will feel duped. So I knew that the budget was going to be pretty expensive and that we would need twenty to thirty million dollars to make the film properly.'

At Working Title, moves were set in motion to get Nicolas Cage interested in the part – and Bevan and Fellner were fortunate to have an ally at his agency CAA. Over the past few years, along with Liza Chasin who runs their LA office, they had developed a good working relationship with Jenny Rawlings, a junior agent at CAA. The relationship had already borne fruit by bringing Hollywood actors into two Working Title productions – John Goodman into *The Borrowers* and Geoffrey Rush into *Elizabeth*.

'When Jenny read the *Corelli* script she said straight away: "We've got to get Nick Cage into this." But the difficulty with stars at Nick Cage's level is getting them to read the script, particularly when their agents see *us* coming and know they're not going to get their full freight fee. Reading our script was the last thing any agent would want Nick to do because he *might* like it! Anyway, we did get him to read it – and he *did* like it.'

On 21 May 1999, Michell and Loader flew to Los Angeles to meet Nick Cage for the first time. Also on the Virgin Atlantic flight was film *wunderkind* Sam Mendes, on his way back from London to LA to begin editing his first film *American Beauty*. This film subsequently dominated the Oscars in 2000 by scooping five awards, including Best Director for Mendes. 'We had a very nice flight with Sam,' says Loader, 'drinking and gossiping about various projects. We all read each other's scripts on the plane and then had dinner when we arrived in LA.'

Nicolas Cage was unfazed by the demands of playing his character and relished the challenges it brought

At nine o'clock the next morning they went to Nick Cage's Bel Air home, which was originally built for Dean Martin. Cage was in the middle of shooting the comedy *Family Man*, but had the morning off. Over breakfast, they discussed the project.

'It was a very honest discussion,' says Loader. 'Basically, we said: "This is the story: You're going to have to do an Italian accent without sounding like an American; learn to play the mandolin; learn how to sing and conduct – and learn how to be an Italian soldier. More importantly, you're going to have to leave the country because we can't make the film in America – we have to make it in Greece."'

Cage was unfazed by the demands of the role, relishing the challenge of pushing himself to his limits.

'He liked the story, liked the script and thought Antonio Corelli was a great character,' says Loader. 'The bottom line is that while lots of films are made, there aren't that many good scripts out there and parts like the one Nick was being offered don't come along that often. I think he sensed an opportunity ... He was looking for a challenge, the more difficult the better in a way.'

Loader and Michell left the meeting buoyed up by Cage's obvious enthusiasm and certain he was the right man for the part. 'We came away absolutely convinced he could do it and that he'd be great ...'

Cage is the nephew of legendary director Francis Ford Coppola, who directed *The Godfather*. With such strong Italian influences around him, Loader and Michell could be forgiven for making the assumption that the actor spoke Italian.

'I'd always assumed that the Coppola clan was pretty big on Italian when they got together round the dinner table, but apparently not. Nick doesn't speak any Italian! However, we had such a high regard for his talents as an actor that we knew speaking in Italian – and speaking English with an authentic Italian accent – was something he could learn,' says Loader. 'It was just a question of preparation. Our goal at that first meeting was simply to explain to him that if he decided to do the film, we felt he needed to start work, sooner rather than later, on some of the things he would be required to do – like speaking Italian and playing the mandolin. In the event, Nick pretty much asked me to provide him with a mandolin teacher before I even mentioned it. He absolutely understood what was involved, how much preparation it was going to take, and that convinced us he was serious and the right person for the part.'

In many ways, the negotiations between Cage's camp and Working Title were relatively smooth. Because Cage was keen to make the film, he was willing to accept a smaller fee than would normally have been demanded and earned for blockbusters such as *Con Air* and *Gone in 60 Seconds*.

One part of the proposal was, however, problematic for Cage. His personal circumstances concerning the custody arrangements of his son, to whom he is devoted, meant that his being out of the country for extended periods was a serious problem. To get around this, Working Title considered building Iannis's house in a Hollywood studio for the shooting of interior scenes, but that would have meant there would be no view of the sea through the window.

In the event, it was decided that building a Hollywood film set would not make a considerable difference to the amount of time Cage would need to spend on location in Greece, and in July 1999 he withdrew from the production.

Discussions then ensued between Universal Studios, Working Title, Loader and Michell about who should replace Cage. Michell and Loader favoured Johnny Depp. However, over at Working Title, Tim Bevan was not ready to give up so easily on Nick Cage.

JUNE 1943

2nd Wednesday: Three carabinieri came at around 9.00 in the morning and searched the house. Beds, cupboards, everything. They even knocked on the walls with a wooden stick and searched under the cupboards and beds. They found the Greek money of Psychi and took it away but luckily returned it after an hour. I went to Mr Bianco and told him this. He promised he didn't know anything about it and advised me to go to the carabinieri in the afternoon. We were shaken and shocked, not that we had anything to hide however.

Extract from diary of Kate Iakovatou-Tool

Corelli and Pelagia on Myrtos Beach

CAPTAIN CORELLI'S MANDOLIN

'Nick won hands down in terms of fire-power and star-power, so we pursued a very long seduction process,' he says. 'Stacey Snider, Chairman of Universal Pictures, and I did a flanking operation to seduce Nick back into the picture. One night I said to Stacey that I wanted to have another crack at getting Nick to do it. She said it would never happen. I said: "No? Rubbish. He liked this part and pulled out of it for all the wrong reasons." So, I just started to bug Richard Lovett, who runs CAA and who is Nick's agent, by phoning him up every night and saying: "Listen, I think Nick should do this . . ."'

Some people might have regarded this as a high-risk strategy: that Cage's agent would become so irritated he would refuse Bevan's calls, but Bevan sees his tenacity as an asset. 'I've learned that tenacity pays, that we need to be more tenacious than anybody else – that if we just keep at it, nine times out of ten we will get a result.'

Bevan's hunch that the part of Corelli was too good an opportunity for Cage to miss – and that his agent would see that – paid off.

'They knew it was a good part. Guys like Nick go around all the time doing films where they fire guns and get their twenty million bucks, but to get a part that stretches them, a part that's really dramatic and has a great director – well, that doesn't happen often. So I knew I was playing a fairly fine deck of cards.'

Captain Corelli and Captain Weber await the surrender of the Greeks

Almost seven weeks to the day that Cage had withdrawn from the film, Loader and Michell flew back to LA to meet him again, this time on the set of *Gone in 60 Seconds.* By then, Cage had already made some arrangements that would enable him to cope with his personal circumstances and travel to Greece to make the film.

Loader and Michell then travelled back to London – but not before Loader had met and arranged a mandolin and Italian teacher for Cage, who was now firmly committed to the project.

φ φ φ φ

Filming was set for April 2000 and the production team was being assembled. Designers were already working on sets at Shepperton Studios, Middlesex, film editor Mick Audsley and costume designer Alexandra Byrne had been signed up and visits were being made to Corfu and Cephallonia for research purposes and to recce locations.

On 30 September 1999, Loader and Michell caught the Eurostar from London to Paris to have meetings with prospective composers and cameramen. On the journey to Waterloo station, Michell had mentioned he felt unwell but had insisted he'd feel fine on the train.

'When we were on the train he seemed OK,' Loader recalls. 'But when we got to the other end – because we had been sitting at the very back of the train – we had to walk the long distance from the end of the train to the foyer of the Gare du Nord. Roger just said: "Something is not right. I feel *really* odd." He had to sit down. By the time we got to the foyer, he realized he was definitely not all right. He was scared – didn't really know what was happening.

'Then he told me he had that tingly arm thing that's always such a give-away. I said: "Roger, that's really worrying. That's a definite heart problem symptom. We should go to a hospital right now in Paris." He said: "I don't want to do that. I'll be three hours away from home and it'll be impossible for the kids . . . Let's just get back on the train."

'We had the most awful train ride back,' says Loader. 'We both thought he was about to have a heart attack at any moment – and on the way I phoned to arrange for a car to pick us up and take us straight to the Royal Free Hospital. When they did a scan and other tests, they found that Roger had had a heart attack the day before. He said he had been feeling a bit odd when he'd picked up his daughter from school the previous afternoon, that he'd gone to bed feeling odd and woken up feeling odd. So by the time he got to hospital it had been over twenty-four hours which is not great because it means that one bit of his heart had been starved of oxygen for twenty-four hours . . .'

Loader and Working Title's Tim Bevan told Michell to put the film out of his mind and rest; that they would then chat again in a couple of months. What he needed most was to take it easy and recuperate, but, understandably, Michell was intensely frustrated.

'We went into an agonizing ten-week limbo,' Loader recalls. 'Obviously – because it was only September and we weren't shooting until April – we hoped Roger would be well enough by then to do the movie.'

By this stage, however, Bevan had come to the conclusion that Michell would not recover in time to make the film.

'I kind of knew instantly that Roger was off the movie,' he says candidly. 'But it was one of those situations where one had to give Roger the space to arrive at that decision himself. He is a personal friend of Kevin's and mine, and because of the sensitivity of the situation, the decision, given that we were already locked into a start date, probably took longer than it should have done. We had a lot of people working on the picture, had pay or play on Nick Cage, and were a couple of million bucks into pre-production. But it was one of those situations where we didn't know for sure how serious Roger's condition was.'

In the interim, Loader held the fort, liaising with scriptwriter Shawn Slovo and production designer Jim Clay.

'Then we got to the end of November and Roger still wasn't sure whether he was going to be able to come back and do the movie. The poor man was in agony: he didn't want to let us down and didn't want to give up the movie, but

Modern buildings on Cephallonia meant it was not the film-makers' first choice

his health had to come first. He's got two young kids – and, after all, it's only a movie. It's not worth killing yourself for.'

On 14 November, Roger Michell decided he could not risk his health and direct the film on the current schedule, which had to remain intact because Nick Cage was already booked up for the rest of 2000.

'It was very disappointing,' says Loader. 'Roger had put so much time and effort into the film. Not only that – there was no guarantee the picture would survive his absence. It was a nightmare.'

Because a film is by nature a vision of the director, it requires the director to be involved in all the pre-planning. As a result, few directors are capable of coming on to a film at a late stage of production and even fewer would want to.

Likewise, in these circumstances, any incoming director also inherits the star who has been chosen. In Nick Cage's case, his contract also gave him approval over the director.

'So the new director had to be someone Nick felt he could work with, someone the studio and financiers felt was capable of directing a $45 million film and somebody Tim and I felt comfortable with culturally – someone who could make a good job of the movie. *Corelli* is very particular material – romantic, funny, moving and epic – and we needed more than just a jobbing director to direct all that.

Despite the 1953 earthquake which devastated the island a few original buildings remain

'We needed someone with a special combination of qualities – and a passion for the film. But one of the consequences of this is that we would have to allow any new director to make the film his own. You can start with the same book, the same screenplay, but once a director starts work they'll take it in radically different directions.

'Kevin and I both wanted a European director to do the picture,' says Tim Bevan. 'We just knew from the beginning that it should be a quintessentially European movie.'

One man who had all the qualities needed – combined with an impressive track record, and the ability to retain the confidence of the American studios which were providing much of the film's funding – was English director John Madden. He had enjoyed a huge success with *Shakespeare in Love* – which had dominated the 1999 Oscars by winning seven, including Best Picture – and the highly acclaimed *Mrs Brown*. At the time of the *Corelli* crisis, he was developing two new projects for Miramax, but fortunately neither of these was ready to go into production in the spring.

On 14 November 1999, a copy of the script was sent to John Madden, with Roger Michell's blessing.

'From John's point of view, the biggest worry was the time factor,' says Loader. 'Would he have time to work with Shawn to get the script into something he felt was more personally his own vision of the material, rather than Roger's vision, or Louis de Bernières' book version?'

Aside from the changes to the script, Madden would also have to make some speedy decisions on set design and wardrobe.

'It was a very tall order for someone to come on at that notice,' says Loader. 'But John decided he could do it, which was the best possible news and incredibly lucky for us. I couldn't think of anyone better.'

There were, however, other complications to surmount. Madden was signed to American film giant Miramax in an exclusive three-film deal.

'I had set our picture up with our two partners, Universal and Canal-Plus, neither of which was predisposed to work with Miramax,' says Bevan. 'But it was one of those situations where when John read the script, he said: "Yes, I love it, but I want to do a lot of work on it . . ." He was committed to it, but we knew there was a pretty huge mountain to get over if we were to get the backers to fall in line behind the new approach.'

Bevan was determined that Madden was the right man for the job.

'Right from the first conversation, I felt John would take the film to a level I always felt it could be taken to. He wasn't afraid of shaking things up – inventing – bringing in a new story to the piece . . . It was what the film was crying out for and it was very exciting.'

φ φ φ φ φ

'Directing is all about finding a piece of material that excites you – and, obviously, the range and richness of the *Corelli* material, and indeed the contrast in tone, was incredibly attractive,' says John Madden. 'You don't often find material that has the kind of scope that encompasses humour, almost farce at times, and tremendous emotional depth and pain, and so on.'

However, as Madden explains, there were some key changes he wanted to make to the script: 'The book's strengths are manifold and obvious. It's a fantastically rich, dense text and I salute Roger, Kevin and Shawn for having taken on the tough job of adapting it in the first place . . . The fantastic richness of characters, wonderful sense of atmosphere, very strong sense of *mise-en-scène* were clear in the script I read, but I felt the material needed to be organized differently for film . . .

'What was needed, I felt, was a narrative shape rather than simply a sequence of marvellously entertaining, psychologically true moments strung out, like beads on a necklace . . .

'One of the pleasures of the book, I think, is that you can pick it up, put it down, then pick it up again two weeks later, and still immediately hook into the atmosphere of it. It isn't propelled by a sequential narrative.'

Madden saw the character of Pelagia as central to both the book and the film.

'It is Pelagia's film and her relationship with the two men – Mandras and Corelli – affect her in different ways,' he says. 'Although the title of the book – and the film – is *Captain Corelli's Mandolin,* she is the emotional core of the story, with her father, Dr Iannis, standing in as the third man in that emotional configuration.'

As such, Madden felt that the drama in the film would be enhanced by the addition of a meeting between Corelli and Mandras.

'Clearly – in the sense that this woman feels herself divided between two men – it is a triangular love story. And in the book she is literally divided between the two men because they never meet. In addition, a tantalizing piece of history is that the Italians on Cephallonia and the partisans *did* collaborate during confrontations with the Germans, and the partisans were given weapons. The moment I knew that to be fact, it opened up the possibility of making Pelagia the centre of the story.'

John Madden also wanted to change the end of the film. De Bernières' ending which saw Corelli and Pelagia reunited in their seventies, after fifty years

Director John Madden and Nicolas Cage discuss the next scene while on location in Sami

had passed, he felt, would be almost impossible to do successfully on film and would detach the audience emotionally, in that the now aged Corelli and Pelagia would not look realistic if the actors were 'aged' with make-up or if they were played by different actors. To keep to the book's ending, Madden decided, would be – in movie terms – 'a form of suicide'.

All script problems aside, there were still some serious contractual hurdles to overcome before Madden could sign up for the film.

'Miramax didn't want to release him,' says Tim Bevan. 'They wanted half the financial returns of the picture. But they couldn't because I'd already given the whole picture to the people who were backing us.'

The negotiations with Miramax's legendary boss Harvey Weinstein were fraught.

'It was tough,' says Bevan, 'but I've been through a lot of battles with Harvey. He plays hard but he's a great enthusiast and he loves European films. Cinema has been the better off for having him around for the last ten or fifteen years – I like the guy a lot.

'I don't have a problem with him being in on the picture at all and at the end of the day he released John and he got a good price for it. The thing about films and the film business is there are big battles that you fight, but you win them or lose them and then you move on.

'Having Harvey on board if the film is any good is great, as he's the greatest proponent and supporter of a decent movie anywhere. He's brilliant at just telling the world that it's great. He's a big character and people listen to him.'

Having Madden aboard was a great boost, but time was very much of the essence. Madden threw himself wholeheartedly into the film.

'Nick Cage's commitment to the project meant that the dates were pre-dictated by his availability. There was a huge job to be done on the script but, stupidly, at the time my feeling was: "Well, we'll get to where we get to, and then if we've got problems we'll see how we can solve them." In my mind, I suppose there was always the possibility that I'd be able to move Nick's other commitments forward because he'd become so incredibly excited about the project.'

Meanwhile, production designer Jim Clay had arrived on Cephallonia on 1 December 1999 and was proposing that they switch all the filming to this island and cancel plans to shoot substantial sections in Corfu. He desperately needed a decision from the director because, in order to meet the April shooting deadline, construction work on the sets had to begin in a matter of weeks.

On 12 December, despite not having formally signed a deal to make the film, Madden flew to Cephallonia to meet Clay, and recce Sami, a town on the east coast of the island, and other possible locations. Three days later he, Loader and Clay flew to Corfu by helicopter in torrential rain to see the village of Perithia. Six days later, Madden was back in London to meet Spanish actress Penélope Cruz, who was being considered for the part of Pelagia.

Over Christmas, Madden worked on the script with Shawn Slovo and Irena Brignull who Madden had asked to join the project as a script editor.

'We were working under fantastic pressure to find the creative space in which to re-imagine the script without having to clip our wings or limit our imagination because of the requirements of the schedule breathing down our necks. That made it very anxiety-inducing,' Madden recalls.

On 10 January 2000, John Madden and Kevin Loader flew to Los Angeles so that Madden could meet Nick Cage for the first time, have a second meeting with Penélope Cruz, and meetings with executives from Universal Pictures.

'I think Nick was predisposed to the idea of working with John because he thought *Shakespeare in Love* was a triumph and liked *Mrs Brown* . . . But obviously leading actors and directors usually have to look each other in the eye before they commit.'

'It was an anxious time,' says Madden. 'I was proposing a fairly seismic realignment of the tectonic plates of the story and had to involve Nick in that

From plaster and scaffolding, production designer Jim Clay and his team recreated a world that no longer exists

process. He had committed to a different script and I had to talk him through the changes to make sure he was still interested in making the film. I think he was quite startled when he first saw the new draft, but he treated it with an open mind and, after we had talked about it at great length, he embraced it and became completely committed to it. He needn't have done this. Given the circumstances, he could have walked away.'

'John felt the script needed to bind the principal characters' destinies together in a far more complicated interdependent manner than in the previous script or indeed in the novel,' says Loader. 'The book is a succession of incidents and character moments – which is great – but this doesn't accumulate the kind of emotional weight that's needed for a film audience. If you really want to get them involved, you need to look at this aspect very carefully.

'I think John felt that Corelli was very unrealized in the book – that he was a bit of a chimera of a character. He has no history . . . I think John also felt that the script didn't exploit the triangular nature of the Corelli, Pelagia, Mandras relationship properly. Principally, this was because, in the original draft, we followed the storyline of the book in which Corelli and Mandras never meet because they are rarely on the island at the same time because Mandras is always

Young lovers: Pelagia and Mandras have no idea that their lives are about to change forever

disappearing just as Corelli arrives. John simply looked at this and said it was "inherently anti-dramatic". He said: "Why are we doing it that way? Let's up the ante. Let's make this love affair more difficult to realize." You see, in the book, Corelli and Pelagia have a pretty easy time. There aren't really any emotional obstacles in their way, apart from the fact that the Second World War intervenes.

'For the movie we needed to make Corelli more instrumental in the resistance against the Germans; and needed to introduce a sense of what it was like for him to feel some responsibility for the men in his platoon, so that when he survives the firing squad in which they're all killed, what is the effect of that on him? In the book this kind of fades to nothing – he simply walks away. He does have a difficult convalescence, but it's never really made clear *why* he leaves the island. The notion that it's simply a bit dangerous for him to hang around was always one of the problems in adapting the book, but I don't think that section of the novel was really well drawn in terms of what was going on in Corelli's head. Anyway, as John outlined what he wanted to do with the script, he realized it was going to be an enormous amount of work.'

φ φ φ φ

Another major – and controversial – alteration that John Madden wanted to make to the script was to have Corelli kill Günter Weber – the young German officer with whom Corelli had become friends – something that was still being discussed even after the scene had been filmed. 'That's the change we are arguing about with Louis de Bernières at this very moment,' Kevin Loader said in July 2000, halfway through the shooting of the film. 'And I definitely think Roger would have been in Louis's camp on that – that Corelli would never kill anybody.'

John Madden explains why he wanted to make the change, which ultimately was not included in the final cut: 'Dramatically speaking, I felt there was an open end to the original story. My fundamental feeling, particularly when transcribed into cinematic life, was that the defining event of the film would be the firing squad. And, in film narrative, I believe that you require a dramatic arc – particularly in a story of this emotional intensity.

'So, one of the principles I operated on when approaching the script was to extrapolate the story forwards and backwards from the firing squad and it struck me in particular that, as a character, Corelli lacked a proper arc in the story. He got old in the book but, essentially, aside from being more bruised and muted, he remained the same person after the massacre. I felt that that moment in the story called for development, whereas, according to the book, this is a man who has never raised a weapon in anger against anybody; a man who simply joined the army as many men did at that time, without coming to grips with the reality of what fighting for your fellow men really means.

'It also seemed to me that the Günter Weber strand of the story was left completely unresolved. I felt the story was about friendship – and how the terms

'Heil Hitler!'
'Heil Puccini!'
Captain Weber joins
Corelli and his men on
the beach

"friends" and "enemies" have to be defined in times of war. After all, these two men – Mandras and Corelli – who should be enemies, curiously end up, at least in a military sense, as allies. And, in my version of the story, albeit for completely personal and emotional reasons, Mandras saves Corelli. Likewise, Corelli and Weber, who should in real terms be friends because Weber clearly worships Corelli, actually have to end up fighting for and living by their own ideologies.

'It struck me that there was an extraordinary scene to be had here because I felt that Weber craved deliverance from what is, for him, a journey into hell. It seemed to me to be an extraordinary destination from where their journey started – and a very strong and defining scene. I also felt that when Corelli left the island, he should leave as a ghost – a shattered man – not as somebody who rather wistfully wished he could stay for another glass of retsina and another canoodle in the olive groves with Pelagia. Their relationship, I felt, had to be shattered, blown apart by what had happened to him. And, in weaving all these threads together, that was the conclusion to the story that naturally presented itself to me.'

Other parts of the novel have also been cut or considerably altered for the film. The eccentric British Special Operations Executive man Lieutenant 'Bunny' Warren, for example, who speaks ancient Greek, does not figure in the film at all, nor does Pelagia's beloved pine marten Psipsina.

The film notably also presents a different view of the complex historical controversy which surrounds the role of the Greek partisans, as previously discussed. However as neither film nor book pretends to be primarily a historical document and even first-hand accounts of the period differ, this is hardly surprising.

Arguably the biggest change from the book to the screen is the ending. John Madden explains why he felt it was essential to alter it: 'In the book, the circumstances in which Corelli returns – and the reasons for him staying away – always seemed to me to be inexplicable; based on no satisfactory emotional foundation – only a kind of a coincidence and a mistake in that Corelli came back, thought he wasn't wanted and went away again. I don't think an audience would ever accept that in a movie context.'

Kevin Loader adds: 'John has made some very radical changes, but in other ways they are not radical at all. They just take the logic of the characters that Louis created to a rather more dramatic conclusion than Louis seemed inclined to do. But, arguably, that is what the process of film adaptation requires. And the script is considerably better than the one we started with.'

Loader also believes that once they had Nick Cage attached to the film, the rest of the cast, including Pelagia, could have been made up of unknown actors, with Greeks playing Greeks and Italians playing Italians.

Nicolas Cage: 'Serious about his work', in the words of director John Madden

'If we'd met the perfect Greek girl and she had perfect English then, yes, we might have cast her as Pelagia. But, if you're not a particularly experienced actor, it's a hell of a thing to step into a big movie like this and play the lead opposite Nick Cage. In the event, John suggested Penélope Cruz and that notion became a very, very attractive one.'

John Madden considers Nick Cage's performance as Corelli to be outstanding.

'The idea of a man turned inside out – whose insides are literally ripped out of him – a man we love for his sense of life and his refusal to bow to conventions, is tremendously attractive. This seemed to me to be a part that Nick was uniquely well qualified to play. He's everything a director could wish for in an actor – serious about his work, gives a fantastic amount of thought to preparation – and always brings something to the table. He's also quite uninhibited about ideas – and is always willing to explore the kind of madness and craziness a character requires.

'As an actor, he has a wonderful sense of dignity – a kind of honour – which is crucial to Corelli because that is what Pelagia found so attractive and irresistible about him. Nick is also extraordinarily generous and supportive with other actors, and there was a fantastic chemistry and rapport between him and Penélope. So it was a wholly enjoyable experience.

'Even though he is Italian by blood, he'd never been to Italy nor had to act Italian in quite that way, but he mastered a wonderfully consistent Italian accent very quickly. The fact that he also learned to play the mandolin is typical – absolutely typical of his imagination and application.'

'I'd seen Penélope in three Spanish films, *All About My Mother*, *Open Your Eyes* and *The Girl of Your Dreams*,' says Madden. 'She was someone who'd lodged in my head and just seemed to be right . . . She's Mediterranean and has the extraordinary physical presence that the film needed. She's a very physical actress and her body language is as important as what she says. Penélope has beauty, passion, sexuality, innocence, fragility and strength – all contradictory qualities that are prerequisites for a leading actress.

'Since the core of the film is based on the Pelagia character, I had to have somebody who could occupy that central place with utter emotional authenticity. The fact that Penélope is separated from the majority of the movie-making world linguistically – meaning that English is not her first language – just helped to bed her into Pelagia's world. She's a very instinctive

John Madden describes Penélope Cruz as 'a very instinctive actress'

CAPTAIN CORELLI'S MANDOLIN

actress. For a twenty-six-year-old, she has an incredible emotional maturity, wisdom and *gravitas* . . . and the febrile inner life which the part needs. She also has another extraordinary quality – the ability to span the ages of seventeen to forty without the aid of any make-up whatsoever. Casting is always a hunch and that was the case with Penélope. I felt the role completely belonged to her, and the film triumphantly vindicates that.'

When it came to the part of Dr Iannis, Michell and Loader felt that casting a Greek actor would be problematic: 'One of the difficulties of the Greek acting community is that the older actors don't speak English,' says Loader. 'But, from the beginning, John Madden thought that John Hurt was right for Iannis's part and, the minute he said this, it seemed right. We thought: "Yes, of course . . . *of course* it's John Hurt. How stupid. Why didn't we think of that before?" '

'The idea of John Hurt for Iannis was like an arrow that went straight to its target,' says Madden. 'It struck me that he and Penélope would make a wonderful pair even though they are not the same nationality.' He adds: 'John looks like a man who's lived in the sun most of his life, and he also has a slightly elastic age quality which means that he could be, quite plausibly, Pelagia's father at forty-five and then age as the story goes on. Mainly, though, Iannis is the soul of the island and the film, and John is blessed with an incredible humanity and an extraordinary voice which sounds as if it has lived through a dozen earthquakes and somehow come out bearing the experiences of all of them.'

Christian Bale was suggested as a possibility for Mandras by his agent and had prepared for his interview with John Madden by perfecting an authentic Greek accent. 'We landed on our feet with Christian,' says Tim Bevan. 'John Madden phoned me up one day and said: "[Casting director] Mary Selway has

'The idea of John Hurt as Iannis was like an arrow that went straight to its target,' says John Madden

just told me to go and meet Christian Bale so I'll do it." Then he phoned me up an hour later and said: "I've just cast Christian Bale as Mandras!"'

The rest of the casting was then completed with the addition of Irene Papas – a veteran icon in Greek cultural life and someone known to British and American audiences for Hollywood films such as *Anne of a Thousand Days*, in which she co-starred with Richard Burton, and *The Guns of Navarone* – as Drosoula; David Morrissey – fresh from success in the acclaimed biopic *Hilary and Jackie* – as Weber; newcomer Piero Maggio as Carlo; Greek actors Michalis Giannatos as Kokolios, and Gerasimos Skiadaresis as Stamatis; plus ten talented young Italian actors as La Scala boys.

φ φ φ φ φ

On Friday, 5 May 2000, the cast began assembling on Cephallonia. John Hurt arrived first, followed, two days later, by sixteen other actors, including Nicolas Cage and Christian Bale, who flew in with members of the production team who would be vital for the rehearsals that would take place during the following fortnight. What Nick Cage calls 'Camp Corelli' then came into being.

A rehearsal schedule usually lists the times that actors spend with directors interspersed with costume fittings. A glance at the rehearsal schedule for *Captain Corelli's Mandolin* makes it clear just what diverse activities took place before the cast were ready to step in front of the camera. On Monday, 8 May, Nick Cage began rehearsing with John Madden at a butcher's shop on Karavomylos Road, Sami, while John Hurt went through dialogue with dialogue coach Joan Washington.

In the afternoon while Nick Cage was having a costume fitting at the Athina Hotel, Christian Bale was having fishing lessons from marine co-ordinator James Wakeford. Meanwhile, over at the Aroccaria nightclub, musical director Paul Englishby was putting the actors who make up La Scala through their repertoire of songs before Nick Cage arrived to practise the mandolin with him and mandolin teacher John Parichelli.

The following afternoon, after a morning of acting rehearsals with John Madden and a second costume fitting, Cage joined the La Scala boys for two hours of military drill training at the Sami camping grounds, followed by two hours of singing rehearsals at the Aroccaria nightclub. This sort of schedule continued for another eight days. Then early on Thursday, 18 May, principal photography began with the scene of Mandras fishing off the beautiful Horgota beach.

It had been a long – at times difficult – process just to get to that stage. But now all the elements – cast, director, script, crew and location were in place – and the shooting of *Captain Corelli's Mandolin* had commenced.

Christian Bale as Mandras. He had perfected a Greek accent even before he secured the role

Chapter 3

ANOTHER TIME, ANOTHER PLACE

'Until I started work on the film I had no idea of the slaughter that had taken place on Cephallonia. Here we were standing in this mythical biblical landscape of overwhelming beauty only to be told that thousands of Italians and Greeks had been massacred here in four days. It was astonishing – unbelievable – that any human being could do that to other human beings anywhere in the world . . . But, somehow, in such a beautiful landscape, it seemed even more incredible. Cephallonia looks like paradise now, but it was hell on earth then.'

Jim Clay, Production Designer

The 1953 Cephallonia earthquake killed more than 600 people, devastated the island, and destroyed centuries of historic and beautiful buildings. Today, there are remnants of pre-earthquake Cephallonia still standing, but these are generally very sad monuments to those who lost their lives – mere shells of stone cottages standing high up on hillsides or scattered forlornly in olive groves.

For the film-maker, wishing to depict wartime Cephallonia, it was obvious from the start that the island could not be used because, as with eighty per cent

The young men of Cephallonia depart the island as war between Greece and the Axis forces grows closer

Realism was vital to the production and where possible salvaged materials were used in the construction of the set

of the buildings on the island, the main town, Argostoli, had been reduced to rubble by the earthquake. And what had been built to replace it – although not lacking in some architectural merit – was functional and sadly nothing like the elegant Venetian designs of the past.

With nowhere on the island, then, which resembled wartime Argostoli – a key location in *Captain Corelli's Mandolin* – shooting the film in Cephallonia seemed out of the question.

'Nevertheless, we thought we'd better go and see what the island and landscape looked like so that we could find a match for it elsewhere in Greece,' says producer Kevin Loader.

In March 1998, Loader flew to Athens with Jane Frazer, who was then the head of production at Working Title, to meet prospective Greek associate producers. After this, they flew to Argostoli, the capital of Cephallonia, to be met by an unexpected welcoming committee.

'One of the people we had met the day before had tipped off the Cephallonians that we were coming and we were greeted at Argostoli airport by local dignitaries, including the mayor of Argostoli and the nomarch – the prefect of the island in charge of local government. The only person missing from this impromptu group was the chief of police and it turned out – although no one mentioned this while we were on the island – that the reason he was absent was because two Britons had been found murdered in their beds by two Albanians with pitchforks. Apparently, this was the first murder on the island since the Second World War massacre of the Italians. I'm sure that's not altogether true, but it's what people were saying at the time . . . and today's Cephallonia is a very crime-free, non-violent place.'

The trip confirmed Loader's view that, given the modern architecture, it would be impossible to use the island for filming. The only crumb of comfort he could offer the island's dignitaries was that it might be possible to film some landscape and beach shots there.

In addition to the beaches and landscape, the film required three other key locations: Old Argostoli, which needed to have Venetian architecture and a deep-sea waterfront; Mandras's village, which needed to be close to the sea; and Iannis's and Pelagia's home, which, ideally, needed to have the sea clearly visible from its windows.

The location for Argostoli also needed to be sealed off from public view and access while the filming was in progress – particularly when the battle sequences were taking place. The practicalities of this meant that any village which had a through-road would be extremely problematic because halting traffic while filming would be impossible if – as was likely – the road was the only route round the island. 'We really needed to find a village that was a dead end,' says Loader.

After Cephallonia the next port of call was Corfu, a suggestion which had come from Susie Tasios, their newly recruited associate producer. She sent Loader a large packet of photographs, and Perithia, a small village in northern Corfu, caught his eye as a possible village location. 'It was quite inland, but you could see the sea from it and it was rather magical,' he says.

Corfu Town, a pretty Italianate town, also appeared to fit the bill for Argostoli. 'It is much maligned by its reputation as a tourist destination,' says Loader. 'But if it was in Italy, it would be a very famous spot like Lucca or Bologna. It's very beautiful, and had some fantastic locations for us – backstreets and lots of little Venetian nooks and crannies.'

What it did not have, however, was a waterfront of the appropriate scale for the film.

'We'd settled on the village in Corfu – and knew we could do some back-street shooting in Corfu Town – but we couldn't find the right configuration of waterfront and sea in Corfu Town because it is so built up and fortified.'

The striking landscape of Cephallonia

They decided to widen their search for the location for Argostoli, and looked at almost every other Venetian port in Greece; they even went to Crete, which has another wonderful Venetian port, Hania. Finally, in December 1998, the tourist port of Sami, on the eastern side of Cephallonia, came into view during a recce. Kevin Loader, Susie Tasios and Stuart Craig, who was to have been the film's production designer, were returning from Ithaca to the Greek mainland when the ferry put in at Sami.

'I remember Stuart getting off the ferry to buy some film. And, when he came back, he said, "You'll think I'm insane, but I think we could film the waterfront here because there are buildings I can either clad or adapt and make a Venetian waterfront without having to spend too much money." Susie and I looked at the four rather square concrete buildings in front of us and thought: "He has gone mad!"'

Nevertheless, after taking a closer look at Sami, it was decided that Perithia could be used for the village, Corfu Town for Argostoli and the Sami waterfront as the Argostoli waterfront. This decision was then supported by Jim Clay, who joined the team as Production Designer when Stuart Craig had to leave the project to work on a previous commitment to Robert Redford's film *The Legend of Bagger Vance.*

φ φ φ φ φ

In August 1999, Jim Clay and a small team arrived in Corfu and began measuring and surveying Perithia, and working out which houses would need re-roofing and repairing. It soon became clear that it wasn't going to be a cheap exercise.

'We were very taken with Corfu Town and its original Venetian architecture,' says Clay, an unassuming, down-to-earth Yorkshireman. 'It's romantic and organic and seemed to me to suit the atmosphere of the piece.'

But the practical problems of filming there quickly began to surface. 'Corfu Town is attractive and still appears to be unspoilt, but it's also a thriving, commercial, cosmopolitan town that's punctuated with branches of Barclays Bank, Kookaï, Armani and The Body Shop. To take over all those – buy them out for four or five weeks while we shot the film – was impossible.'

In addition, many of the modern roofs would either need to have been replaced – which would have been extremely expensive – or covered.

Finally, it was decided that rather than shoot on two separate islands, everything should be filmed on Cephallonia. And, instead of trying to find an existing pre-earthquake village, a film set should be built from scratch. Then, following careful negotiations with the mayor and business people in Sami, a town square set would be built in a way that would hide the modern buildings.

This approach would also give the production team another useful benefit – almost total control of the village where they were shooting. 'Having such control is vital to the success of any movie staying on schedule,' says Clay.

The decision to shoot the film on Cephallonia was a collaborative one, but its key advocates were Jim Clay and John Madden.

'Filming in two places – Corfu and Cephallonia – seemed to be asking for trouble,' says Madden. 'It would have denied us flexibility, and we would have ended up with split construction crews and the difficulty of moving the crew from one place to another. Although the team had found a rather magical location for the village in Corfu, this site actually presented us with more than we needed in construction terms. It was too big and, more significantly, had no clear relationship with the sea which, I felt, was vital to reminding us that the film was set on an island.'

The sets were so realistic that few tourists would have realized that the buildings were fakes

According to producer Tim Bevan, shooting the film in one, rather than two locations proved to be the right decision in more ways than logistics: 'It actually proved to be an economical way of doing it,' he says. 'It would have been more costly to split locations, to do the studio stuff in England or somewhere else in Europe and the location stuff in Greece or America. The location that was decided on was like a backlot that happened to be on the Ionian Sea!'

φ φ φ φ φ

The Cephallonians who had welcomed the advance party of Kevin Loader and Jane Frazer in March 1998 could not really have appreciated what an impact the shooting of the film would have on their island. In purely economic terms it generated millions of pounds in fees for locations, rental of apartments, hotel rooms – and petrol – in addition to the future benefits of a huge increase in tourists once the film had been released.

The film company also rented so many hire cars on the island that extra cars had to be shipped over from the mainland for 'ordinary' tourists when the holiday season began. Block bookings of hotel rooms for cast and crew were made months in advance, and local restaurants suddenly found they had an influx of guests, all with cash in their pockets and an eagerness to relax after long days of filming.

Director John Madden outside the *kapheneion*

Many of the cast and crew stayed in Aghia Efimia, about twenty minutes' drive from Sami, and one islander had the foresight to change his bar's name to 'Corelli's', to ensure that it would appeal to the next season's tourists and continue the bumper takings that had been generated by the film crew drinking there.

Ironically, despite the fact that the film company had to pay for accommodation and food for the cast and crew, Tim Bevan thinks that being on an island actually helped to keep production costs down.

'Making *Captain Corelli's Mandolin* is the most ambitious thing our company has done, but I think we went about it in the right way because when you're isolated – as we were on Cephallonia – everything has to be on hand and people make a mental commitment to being there,' he says. 'Fringe expenditure is not an option. You can't just wake up to a need, reach for a phone and fly something in on the day because it just wouldn't get there on time. Everything has to be pre-planned.

'By scheduling the filming in chunks, so that you tackle a battle chunk and then another chunk, means that all the resources have to be lined up, present on the spot. There is no way you can go outside these resources. Whereas if you're shooting at Shepperton Studios, England, you can, because you just pick up the phone and somebody sends it. And that's how the trickle-down factor and expenditure goes up and up.'

φ φ φ φ

With the problem of the location solved, another difficulty became apparent. Nick Cage, the star of the film, needed to back in Hollywood by the end of July to start work on another project. So, instead of some of the *Corelli* sets being built while filming was taking place on other sets, all the sets needed to be constructed simultaneously.

'All the scenes involving Nick had to be shot upfront,' says Kevin Loader, 'so we had to get all the Argostoli scenes, all the battle scenes, and a big bulk of the village scenes done in the first seven or eight weeks of a twelve-week shoot.'

At the same time, Jim Clay, John Madden, and director of photography John Toll – who won Oscars for his work on *Braveheart* and *Legends of the Fall* – began looking for the perfect location to build the village.

'We drove around the island just looking for an area where we could actually believe the village might have grown,' says Clay. 'But what we were up against was the picture-postcard beauty of Cephallonia. And that was John Toll's major worry when he arrived on Cephallonia. His first concern was how blue the sky was, how green the landscape, how cobalt blue the sea, and how all that could destroy the atmosphere of the film and make it look as if a set had simply been placed on top of the landscape. So we chose areas that were not quite so green and lush, and areas which had a dustier feel, so that our

Production designer Jim
Clay's watercolour ideas
for the set. (Below)
Argostoli and (opposite,
above) the doctor's
house with (inset) the
final version

architecture could settle down into the landscape and look as if it had grown there. The site we ultimately chose for the village was a hilly terraced area where we could settle the whole thing in – and, just as we had hoped, the village did look as if it had always been there.'

The site chosen was Dihalia, a small peninsula, just outside Sami, which is reached by a long winding road that eventually ends at Antisamos Beach. The beach is popular with locals and tourists, but the mayor of Sami agreed to close the road to traffic while filming was taking place. The film company then organized a regular bus service to take the holiday-makers and locals to and from the beach.

'Dihalia is a sliver of land with the sea on either side, which was something John Madden was keen to have,' says Jim Clay.

For Clay the *Corelli* film was a challenging and thrilling project. 'Venice is one of my favourite cities in the world – and here I was faced with the enormously exciting opportunity to create a Venetian style of architecture for a movie.'

Drawing on a range of reference material gathered from personal visits to similar towns, and from books, pictures and photographs, Clay began sketching his ideas for the sets of Old Argostoli and the village.

'It was an interesting and exciting time because it is a different architectural vernacular to the one I am used to,' he says. 'As a production designer, you do an awful lot of English Edwardian and Victorian interiors and exteriors – and a lot of contemporary work – but, clearly, this was neither of these. What we were basing the sets on was a beautiful, organic, human style of architecture.'

Clay thought that a subtle but important part of the film was that, in sharp contrast to the horror of the German atrocities, wartime Cephallonia was a place of great history and beauty.

'Until I started work on the film I had no idea of the slaughter that had taken place on Cephallonia,' he says. 'Here we were standing in this mythical biblical landscape of overwhelming beauty only to be told that thousands of Italians and Greeks had been massacred here in four days. It was astonishing – *unbelievable* – that any human being could do that to other human beings anywhere in the world . . . But, somehow, in such a beautiful landscape, it seemed even more incredible. Cephallonia looks like paradise now, but it was hell on earth then.'

Resisting the temptation to make the locations in the film look too much like a picture postcard was a direction that came from the top downwards.

'*Corelli* was never going to look like a rich film because at the time in which the novel is set, Cephallonia was not a rich environment,' says John Madden. 'At that time it was all the faded glory of the Venetian empire really – and obviously that architectural landscape does not exist any more because of the earthquake.

'It was a place which had faced the ravages of time – and damp weather. One is inclined to think of Greece only in its summer mood because that is most people's experience of it, but the winters there are hard – very wet –

discoloured – and moss grows on everything. Jim and I were working within a fairly monochromatic range, in order to control the palette of the film so that it didn't explode into romantic Technicolor.

'I felt that the romance of the story was a very important part of the movie, but that this had to be balanced against a certain kind of reality so that when the war engulfs the characters it doesn't simply feel like a Hollywood manipulation – because, to some extent, this kind of story is familiar territory as far as movies are concerned.'

As production designer, Clay's job is to visualize the whole film, working closely with the director, the director of photography and the costume designer. At the peak of *Corelli*, he had a team of 350 people working for him and a budget of $4 million.

'Along with the others, it's my job to set the style and look right at the beginning. Having decided how the physical space will work in relation to the camera and action, the texture and palette – which I guess sets the atmosphere for the film – is added. From then on, you become the architect who has to turn that broad concept into a three-dimensional space for people to work in.'

(Opposite and below) From Jim Clay's sketches sets were transformed into physical reality

Building the Argostoli
set meant major
upheaval for the people
of Sami and
necessitated the
removal of an electricity
sub-station

One key scene, early in the movie, requires the Italian Army to arrive and disembark from a port and, for this action, the team finally decided on Sami as the location to double for Argostoli. In addition to the port, a town square was also needed – and there was, as already mentioned, one, of sorts, in Sami. Although this was modern, unattractive – and, unfortunately, featured an electricity sub-station slap-bang in the middle along with some electricity poles – its major plus was that it was barely a few hundred yards from the harbour front which would enable some scenes to be done in one complete landscape shot.

Having gained the general support of the mayor of Sami, specific negotiations had to begin with the shopkeepers, businesses and hotels that would be affected by the major construction work that would eventually turn modern Sami into wartime Argostoli. When it came to road closures and the turning off of the whole town's electricity supply while the sub-station was moved, the goodwill of all the towns-people would be needed. Even Sami's drains needed to be diverted, as did the disembarkation route for cars coming off the ferry.

'When a film production first arrives in a place people get very excited and want us there,' says Clay. 'Then, as the reality of what we are going to do impacts on them, they have second thoughts. That, classically, was what happened as we moved in and began to explain the sorts of area we needed to take over, what we were going to build and how it would affect their commercial and social life. Ninety per cent of people wanted us there, five per cent saw us as a big profit-making opportunity, but the other five per cent didn't want their island destroyed by the post-film release tourism and were sceptical about the whole project anyway. It took time to work through all that, but we did eventually get everyone on our side.'

Fortunately shooting was to be done throughout the spring to early summer, a time when Sami and the surrounding areas were expected to be relatively free from tourists. This was vital because not only would crowds of passersby and spectators encroach on the filming, but the 'Kastro', Sami's tourist hotel, would be re-fronted with cleverly built sets and taken over by the film crew as its production office. To serve this function, the Kastro's beds would be removed and computers, faxes and photocopiers moved in instead.

Meanwhile, Jim Clay's designs had begun to take shape in sketch and broad concept form, known in the film business as mood boards.

'This was really just charting the visually emotional journey that we were going to take from the calm, sophisticated place that Argostoli must have been before the earthquake,' says Clay. 'The architecture then was spectacular and the landscape overwhelming. Argostoli had its own theatre, dress

shops and was a trading port. When it came to doing my designs, I also mixed in a bit of Corfu. I began sketching what our film world would look like: the life of a busy market town contrasted with the much simpler way of life in the village.'

Detailed models were made and the proposals shown to John Madden. Once he had approved these, Clay's team of draughtsmen turned his sketches into architectural technical drawings. Then, along with the rest of the team, supervising art director, Chris Seagers, began to turn Clay's concept into reality. 'Chris's job was to organize the whole thing, control the budget, crew up with draughtsmen and other art directors, and run the department,' says Clay.

Two other key members of the production were construction manager John Bohan who, with a team of up to 320 carpenters and craftsmen, physically built the set, and set decorator John Bush whose job it was to turn bare plaster walls into what looked like a vibrant living town and village.

In Dihalia, the building of the village – and Doctor Iannis's house – was far from easy because the whole area is a protected unexcavated archaeological site, and the Greek authorities would not allow the soil to be broken up. This meant that foundations could not be dug even for the tallest building, the *kapheneion* – the bar. Instead the buildings were built with support scaffolding placed at ground level and then weighted with huge two-ton, eight-foot square concrete ballast blocks.

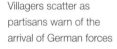

Villagers scatter as partisans warn of the arrival of German forces

In February and March, gale-force winds howl across Cephallonia and, one night after a force eight, the bell tower on the Old Argostoli set became separated from the rest of the building.

'The wind was a worry,' says John Bohan, 'because obviously you can't predict it that easily and we were constructing only temporary buildings ... Force eight is quite a wind.'

The island is also on a geographic fault line and the crew felt several earth tremors during construction work. In February, rain and snow caused difficulties, which was not, says Bohan, something he had expected. And, as spring became summer, the heat presented problems which ranged from a few crew members suffering from heat-exhaustion to the plaster drying too fast, shrinking and falling from walls.

What makes Dihalia so spectacular from a landscape point of view are the steep slopes which drop down both sides of its cliffs but, given the restriction of not being able to build normal foundations, this presented a difficult construction job. 'It was a tricky site to build on,' says Clay. 'The houses, which were built on a scaffold structure, had then to be cantilevered across the slope.'

The doctor's house, where a considerable amount of action was to be filmed, had a few extra requirements that not all the other buildings needed. The intense heat meant that it had to be air-conditioned, which necessitated a five-kilometre electrical cable to be laid from Sami to the village. The interior walls of the house needed to be removable to allow for director John Madden's required camera angles; and outside, a sliding platform – that could be extended or retracted as required – had to be created, so that there would be sufficient space for lights and crew.

'Having lots of different levels in the village was tricky,' says construction manager John Bohan. 'The village set looked much smaller than the Old Argostoli set, but it took longer to build and was definitely more fiddly to construct.'

While the set was being constructed, the island's authorities decided – in order to benefit both the film company and future visitors – to upgrade and widen the road leading to Antisamos.

'This meant we had to arrange certain times to bring lorries up to the set,' says Bohan. 'At other times, we'd ferry people up by minibus and leave them at either side of the road works.'

Sami presented construction problems of a different kind and, when the production team arrived, there was a two-week stand-off between them and some of the shopkeepers who were refusing to sign their contracts. While many had agreed to the sum of compensation offered by the film company for the disruption to their business, others had not, and were holding out for more money. All contracts needed to be agreed before construction of the set could begin.

'Four articulated lorries had arrived from the UK, but we couldn't start constructing anything,' says Bohan. 'Our first task was to build our workshop, but we couldn't even get on with that.'

As negotiations ensued, Bohan, among others, tried to point out the risk that the shopkeepers were taking. 'Over many cups of coffee, I tried to explain to people that we were locked into certain dates to make the film, and it would be made – but maybe not in Cephallonia. That could have happened.'

Some of the shopkeepers, however, just couldn't believe that the film unit would pack up and go elsewhere. In the end, compromises were made and the contracts were signed.

The brinkmanship wrangles over money may have caused consternation among some members of the production team, but it did not particularly surprise Tim Bevan.

'When you have fifty million dollars to spend in a concentrated area outside of, for example, New York, Los Angeles or London, then you're going to get a lot of people sniffing around because that's a lot of money and lots of people want a part of it. So it doesn't matter whether you are dealing with Greek, Italian, American, English, Scottish, Irish or whatever people, you get the same problem.

'If you think about it, the disruption we brought to those people's lives was absolutely monumental – particularly those whose shops had to be closed because we were building outside. They drove a hard bargain, but it wasn't that hard and it all ended up fine.'

A Greek recruiting poster

Over ten weeks, the set began to take shape as construction workers, carpenters and plasterers were drawn from the UK, Athens and Cephallonia. Most of the building materials were shipped in from the United Kingdom, as it proved cheaper to fill huge containers with wood, plaster and paint than buy them in Greece.

The shopping list for the construction work – as the following list shows – was colossal:

- 53,000 metres of scaffold tube (53 kilometres)
- 46,000 scaffold fittings
- 1,000,000 screws
- 750 kilogrammes of nails
- 5,000 sheets of plywood
- 75,000 metres of timber
- 180 tons of plaster
- 150 tons of concrete
- 1,750 gallons of paint

Adding detail to the sets, to transform them from mere shells into authentic, living, breathing buildings, was the job of set decorator, John Bush and a team of props experts. Their task was to scour architectural salvage companies in Athens for original doors, windows, iron gates and shutters – and then, along with the set-dressers, arrange every prop according to Jim Clay's overall concept of how he wanted each set to look.

'This work can involve anything,' Bush explains, 'from pictures, ornaments, knives and forks, and pens, through to tents, ammunition boxes and even the contents of a soldier's pockets – such as family photographs, letters from a girlfriend and an identity card.'

The 1953 earthquake meant there was little pre-war furniture available on Cephallonia that could be used to dress the homes of Dr Iannis and the other villagers. Much had to be brought in from mainland Greece, and the furniture for Iannis's house came from shops in Athens and a flea market in Piraeus.

'We found one or two very interesting bits on the island, but they were few and far between and obviously some people don't want to part with their furniture because it has strong family connections,' says Bush.

Also because Iannis's house is seen in the film being destroyed in the earthquake, the film company needed to own the props and furniture in case they needed to be broken up for that scene. In a perverse way, the earthquake did help

Period detail, right down to individual stamps, was researched for the film

The set built as the home of Dr Iannis even had air conditioning

TEMPO · ΕΛΛΗΝΙΚΗ ΕΚΔΟΣΙΣ ΑΡ. 31-32

ΧΡΟΝΟΣ

Ο "ΜΠΑΛΙΛΛΑ"

ΕΚΤΑΚΤΟΝ ΤΕΥΧΟΣ
ΣΕΛΙΔΕΣ 72   100

Contemporary magazines were reproduced to give homes a realistic feel

with one potentially tricky bit of the set. Part of the inside of the church was to be filmed after the earthquake scene had taken place and the set-dressing team needed, therefore, to recreate the interior. Bush expected that to be a nightmare task, but, in the event, it was not.

'We went to see a pig farmer who lived a few miles from Sami,' Bush recalls. 'He took us round his highly smelly sheds and opened a door to reveal the wonderful decaying remains of a church's interior. By some quirk of fate, the church had stood within an area of his family's land, so when it was decommissioned and stripped he hung on to the furniture. It was a lucky find for us and he kindly agreed to rent us the remains.'

Dr Iannis's house needed to reflect the character's worldliness, but also the simple way of life he lives at a practical level.

'We wanted his house to be culturally opulent but, at the same time, simple,' explains John Bush. 'But there was also a grave danger of slipping into a *House and Gardens'* interior feel because the Mediterranean look is very sought after at the moment. So we had to try and create something that looked as if it had been furnished by Iannis himself, or by his parents.

'It needed to look like a house that had been handed down from his family. There needed to be touches from his wife, who is not featured in the story, and from his daughter, Pelagia. It is very much the doctor's house, but we wanted to combine all those aspects – like, for instance, the small touches of a couple of pictures from Pelagia's childhood that are in the bedroom that Corelli occupies. These are very subtle touches, but one hopes that, in the end, they will create a believable interior.'

Iannis may be financially poor, but he is also well read and his collection of books needed to reflect that. These were purchased at second-hand bookshops in Athens. 'You can't see every single book in the finished film, but we chose them all individually, and the fact that they are there helps – in a sub-conscious way – to create the right atmosphere. There are a lot of Greek medical books and Greek literature and, as Iannis and Pelagia are relatively well educated, there are also classics in foreign languages.'

The Italian posters on the walls of the Argostoli set came from a book on Italian propaganda; and, fortunately, because period posters advertising Greek wine, beer and cigarettes remain popular, these could be easily purchased in Athens. An ephemera dealer in Rome provided items, such as newspapers, magazines, playing cards and pre-printed telegram paper, which could be placed inside soldiers' tents. Part of a set-dressers' job is to second-guess what might be needed even if it is not specified in the script.

Says Bush: 'The script was still undergoing changes when we started our work so we also had to consider various aspects that might crop up. For example, we weren't sure whether there would be scenes in the soldiers' tents and, if so, how much we'd see of their personal possessions. So, when we were buying stuff, we bought items that might be useful. In the event, there was a shot in the script – after the killing-field scene – that involved the looting of the Italian soldiers' possessions, and we obviously had to think of all the things they might have had in their pockets, things that would add to an individual's character.'

No real wartime tents could be found for the Italian military encampment, so these had to be specially made in England and shipped out to Greece. Instead of using Italian designs, the tent-makers copied the design for the tents that had been brought in to house people after the earthquake. These were then dyed to match the wartime colours that were used by the Italians.

The team succeeded in finding more than a thousand wooden Italian ammunition boxes. These were not from the Second World War, but nevertheless fitted the bill and had authentic markings. Other items for the military encampment included large props from oil drums and fire extinguishers to officers' suit bags and chairs.

A key aspect of Jim Clay's vision for the village was that it had to look like a living, breathing place, and great attention was paid to building the houses between existing olive trees and fig trees to give the impression that the trees had grown up around the houses, rather than the reverse. To add to this impression, John Bush and his team planted around 2,000 individual shrubs and bushes alongside the existing trees.

Initial Greek victories over the Italians in Albania were a major boost to morale

'Trying to find well-established plants that could be transplanted and made to look as if they had actually grown there for a long time was tricky. Ideally, months are needed to let everything bed down but, because of the schedules, we did not have that sort of time.'

Another problem with the plants was that they were an instant attraction to the goats – and, eventually, an electric fence had to be erected to keep the animals at bay.

Among the items John Bush's team sourced were:

- 10,000 sandbags, filled, transported and put in place
- 1,200 metres of canvas, dyed to order and made into twenty-seven tents
- 3,000 tent pegs
- 1,000 ammunition boxes imported from Italy
- 320 tons of rubble to create bombed Argostoli
- 2,000 plants

Arguably the most important prop in the film is Captain Corelli's mandolin, Antonia.

'In the book, the mandolin was an old mandolin,' says Bush. 'It was something that had been passed down to Corelli. So we went to a mandolin-maker in Rome, just by the steps of St Peter's, to find one that would fit the bill. We always knew we wanted two, partly because the mandolin is a main prop and having a spare one is sensible, and also because at one time in the story it was going to be buried during the earthquake.

'We found two almost identical antique mandolins, both of which were in need of renovation. We spoke to the mandolin-maker about the sort of decoration he could put on the instruments and he had some lovely original pieces of mother-of-pearl and tortoise inlay. So we hit on a design that he could replicate on the two mandolins and he made them up. He used their original cases, but redid the entire inlay. They have mother-of-pearl all round the edge and a tortoise-shell fret board with mother-of-pearl inlay.

'The mandolins were surprisingly inexpensive – I expected them to cost an awful lot more than he asked for . . . The man who renovated them was in his seventies and you could tell he was a real craftsman who loved his work. He did a great job. I think he was more worried about the cost than we were. He kept on saying: "I don't want to spend too much of your money", and we kept saying: "It's OK – the mandolin is an important prop. It's the title of the film you know! We need it to be the best possible."'

One of two identical antique mandolins used in the film

Because they were antiques, the neck of the mandolin that Nick Cage plays in the film had to be strengthened so that it could cope with tough modern strings and be tuned to the right pitch.

'The mandolins we found are hundreds of years old so they may not sound quite as wonderful as modern ones, but we went for looks rather than sound because we knew that, in the end, the music would probably be played on another instrument.

φ φ φ φ

In addition to building the sets and dressing them, Jim Clay and his team also had to source equipment, such as lorries, tanks and jeeps for the Italian and German armies, and for the landing ships and the ferry which take Mandras and other Greek volunteers off to war.

The seven Italian Fiat Spa lorries and three German army Mercedes trucks were specially built for the film by Plus Film Services, a specialized film action vehicle company, which is run by former oil-rig designer Steve Lamonby. This company can supply the film industry with everything from a modern tank to the Roman catapults used in Ridley Scott's film *Gladiator*.

Using Steve Lamonby's own research material – including original plans collected during a decade of working in films and television and dating back to the beginning of the twentieth century – exact replicas were built in four months at Bray film studios, Middlesex, and then shipped out to Greece.

'Everyone is inclined to assume that there are originals available,' says Lamonby. 'But the problem is – and this was a particular problem with the seven Italian lorries – where do you get a column of sixty-year-old vehicles that all look the same and have an air of uniformity? You can always find one or two, but can't find columns. We also needed to avoid battered old trucks because the vehicles needed to look fairly new as if they had only recently rolled off a military machine production line.'

Fine details on the trucks included authentic markings – and the engines, even if not identical to the originals, had to sound as they would have done during the Second World War.

'A modern diesel engine sounds like a modern diesel engine, and does not smoke like a petrol engine smokes, so we used Ford V8 engines such as those used in vehicles like the Bren Gun Carrier and wartime British lorries,' says Lamonby. The Ford V8s were amazingly reliable and – because they were four-wheel drive and able to tow other vehicles which got stuck – they were also used by the film unit as scout and tow vehicles.'

The two German half-track vehicles used in the film are original wartime ones that Lamonby had in stock. Found originally in wrecked condition in the Czech Republic and Poland, Lamonby and his team restored them. Similarly, the German tank in the film is original and was found in Switzerland.

(Overleaf) Italian troops disembark at Argostoli

The motorcycle used by Nicolas Cage in the film was a veteran of the Second World War

'It is quite probable that all of them saw action during the war,' says Lamonby. 'Quite often when we find vehicles they have shell-holes and machine-gun marks still visible. The German tank we used on *Corelli*, for example, had its original eagles and swastika markings on the gun breach.'

Corelli's motorbike in the film, a Moto Guzzi Alce, is also a wartime original. Based on a successful 1930 racing bike, this model was adapted during the war for military use. Corelli's jeep, a Fiat staff car, is another original wartime vehicle that was supplied via a dealer in Italy. But, as no Italian armoured car could be found, one had to be built from scratch – again using plans from Lamonby's own archive.

'It's an Autoblinder 41,' he explains, 'and that was quite a number to produce. It had to have a turret that turned, a gun that worked, doors that opened and shut – and had to be a four-wheel drive. We built the chassis, and then used some components from British armoured cars.'

The vehicle list also included two German BMW motorcycles and sidecars, and the two other German jeeps, or *kubelwagons*. Sometimes the props, such as the *kubelwagons*, which once again were authentic, bear a grisly reminder of the war.

'You do sometimes wonder what wartime action the vehicles were in,' says Lamonby, 'especially when you see bullet holes in them. One of the *kubelwagons*, for example, has got a bullet hole that enters through the back of the vehicle and goes right through the driver's seat, so I imagine the driver would have been shot.'

CAPTAIN CORELLI'S MANDOLIN

$$\phi \ \phi \ \phi \ \phi$$

James Wakeford, marine co-ordinator, and a former Royal Navy helicopter pilot, had expected to find plenty of authentic wooden fishing boats, or caiques, which could be used as Mandras's boat. He did, but not in an original condition, complete with mast and sail.

'They'd all been modernized and had engines put into them,' he says. 'The owners also wanted ridiculous amounts of money for them. I'd say: "How can you possibly want that much money for this – it's an absolute wreck?", and they'd say: "Ah, that's because it has got a commercial fishing licence." It turned out that the boat itself was worth a thousand pounds, but with a commercial fishing licence it was worth three thousand.'

Eventually Wakeford found two caiques in terrible condition – and made them into one useable boat.

'They were almost in pieces, but it was cheaper to restore them than buy ones that were up and running,' he says. 'Then we had to find the right sail design, and managed to persuade an old fisherman to sell us his old sail.'

Wakeford found another fisherman who could teach actor Christian Bale how to throw a net correctly, while he himself taught the actor how to sail.

German troops demand that the Italians give up their weapons. The half-track pictured was another veteran of the Second World War

'I've taught a fair few people how to sail in my time, but Christian was amazing . . . he just picked it up. He then had to learn the Greek type of rowing – a very important part of the film – which is done standing up.'

Thanks to the efforts of associate producer Susie Tasios, the Greek Navy lent two mine-sweepers to double as Italian corvettes and two fifty-five-metre landing craft to play the Greek and German landing craft, while the Greek coastguard lent patrol craft to keep waterborne sightseers at bay during filming. Because the mine-sweepers had modern radar dishes on their superstructure, they had to be filmed face-on in order not to show their twenty-first-century technology. The same ships were used in the background for the German invasion scene, and the landing ships were repainted with German markings for that scene.

For the scene showing Mandras and other young Greeks going off to war, a ferry was needed. A rare period one was found, but it had no engine and would have needed to be towed everywhere. Eventually a water container ship was hired and Jim Clay's team converted it so that it looked like a ferry.

'It meant virtually building our own ferry, but at least it had an engine and was mobile,' says Clay, 'so those were the deciding factors.'

There were no wartime Stuka aircraft in existence, so the airborne attack scenes were added to the film, using Computer Generated Imagery (CGI), at a post-production phase. The same technology was used to 'paint out' any remaining parts of the modern radar on the mine-sweepers. CGI technology has improved rapidly during the past few years, and is increasingly used to make additions and alterations.

But as Jim Clay's incredible sets for *Captain Corelli's Mandolin* demonstrate, when it comes to realism you cannot beat constructing the real thing. The final proof that the reconstructed 'authenticity' was successful came from locals who visited the Argostoli set. As Jim Clay recalls: 'The most gratifying thing was seeing all these locals – especially the older people – coming around tapping the walls of the film set because they thought it was real.'

One astute Cephallonian printing company even produced several 'Old Argostoli' postcards, without bothering to explain that the images shown were of a film set that would only be there for a few weeks. 'Next year the tourists will be buying these postcards and looking for a place they'll never find,' smiles Clay. There was even a suggestion from a local businessman that he should buy the film set and recreate old Argostoli on land near Sami, but that idea never got off the ground.

'I was told that people who arrived in Sami had no idea they were on a film set,' says construction manager John Bohan.

That is a testament to the work of the production team, which, in using their skills and experience, recreated somewhere that no longer exists. In doing so, they are able to suspend the film-goers' own reality and transport them, through their sets and action, to another time and another place.

Chapter 4

CREATING THE ILLUSION

'Captain Corelli's Mandolin is a saga in the noblest tradition of the genre. Among de Bernières' skills are an archaeologist's eye for place, a historian's feel for time and place and a musician's ear for tone and tempo – the novel has everything and if it does not hold you in its thrall, it might be worth checking to see if your heart is made of stone.'

Jasper Rees, *Daily Telegraph*

The attention to detail paid to the sets and props for *Captain Corelli's Mandolin* is mirrored by that taken to ensure every actor looks and sounds the part, and that the music, which features throughout the film, is authentic. The great expectations raised by the incredible success of the book, the vast scale and range of the film, combined with the sheer number of actors and extras, was a mega challenge for everyone concerned.

Having created 825 uniforms for *Captain Corelli's Mandolin*, costume designer Alexandra Byrne could be forgiven for never wanting to see – or make – a uniform ever again, but that is not the case.

'I started off not knowing anything about uniforms other than ones I had seen on the screen before,' says Byrne, who was nominated for Oscars for her work on the films *Hamlet* and *Elizabeth*. 'I'd never done a war or uniform film before, and the research, logistics and everything that went into it was a challenge.

'I did a lot of research on the Italian uniforms – and, believe me, you can get quite into them! Once I got into the background, it became quite interesting. I tend to work in that way. I need to research and understand everything to be able to make things work in terms of character and clothes, and that's why it's so daunting getting to that point. There are people who live and breathe uniforms, but I don't. I was a beginner – so, for me, it was a huge learning curve.'

Pelagia (Penélope Cruz) gathers herbs in the field

David Morrissey as
Captain Günter Weber

What proved to be most useful for Byrne's research into both the civilian and military clothing were people's personal photographic albums.

'The pictures, for example, showed exactly how people wore their uniforms,' she says. 'And what I found most interesting is that the soldiers personalized their uniforms by putting crucifixes under their collars and by sewing in extra pockets to hold things like watches. They made adaptations for practicality and comfort.'

Having read the research material and examined countless photographs, Byrne flew to Rome. 'I wanted to see if I could dig out some original uniforms – and that's when it became really interesting,' she says. 'Because there is a huge market for original German uniforms, these are usually snapped up by dealers and are quite hard to come by, but there are lots of Italian uniforms around – and we bought a lot of them.

'Typically Italian, there's a kind of Mafia of Italian military experts. After meeting one, a whole network of strange contacts opened up. Word of mouth helped, too. The Italian assistant I was working with was having a new kitchen fitted, and the plumber who came to do it happened to see her reference material and said he knew a man she should go and see. We ended up in garages doing deals with people over old uniforms.'

Perhaps surprisingly, knowing how badly much of the Italian army was equipped – particularly in the ill-fated battles in Albania, as detailed in de Bernières' novel *Captain Corelli's Mandolin* – the officers' uniforms were far from modest.

'Their uniforms are the most extraordinary pieces of tailoring I have ever seen. They are quite beautiful, hand-finished, with great attention to detail. Every one was a one-off for each officer and all the uniforms were different compared to the tailoring of the German uniforms. The logistics of the Italian uniform were really stuck in the First World War, whereas the Germans were an up-and-running, forward-looking, moving-on fighting machine, so their style of tailoring is different.'

The research, says Byrne, whose team numbered forty-six people, working in both Greece and England, helped her in other unexpected ways, too. 'For example, when reading soldiers' letters I discovered that, unlike their officers, ordinary Italian soldiers did not have summer uniforms, and some of them made their own shorts out of tent canvas. So we made some shorts from the same material.'

The fact that ordinary Italian soldiers had no summer uniform was reflected in the film. 'You can see by the sweat on people's faces,' says Byrne, 'that they were dressed in wool and had no summer kit at all, whereas the Germans were very well equipped with the appropriate gear for the conditions they were in.'

Despite being sixty years old, many of the wartime uniforms were still in excellent condition and Byrne and her team bought some to kit out extras, and borrowed others from costume houses. They did, however, encounter one problem – sizes.

'Despite what some people say, people were smaller back then compared to today's big, beefy, gym-bound modern bodies, so many people could not fit into the originals.'

Using officers' uniforms, which may have been worn in action during the war, was something that preoccupied Byrne: 'Sometimes I would look at a uniform and think: "What did your officer see? What did he do?"'

Italian costume houses also had many uniforms, but most of these were for other regiments and could not be easily adapted to suit the 33rd Regiment of Artillery to which Corelli and his men belonged. In addition, Byrne did not feel that some of the modern copies of the uniforms were quite right. 'I prefer originals rather than somebody's interpretation of them,' she says.

The Italian encampment on Antisamos Beach

But because the quantity needed did not match the number of originals available, she decided that the rest would have to be made new. This was done, according to patterns taken from real uniforms, and using 1940s and 1950s cloth.

The uniforms for Nick Cage's Captain Corelli costume, and the La Scala boys and other Italian troops, were specially made in Italy by costume houses which had supply routes to authentic Second World War materials, and tailors who were experienced in making military uniforms.

Signor Russo, the tailor who made Nick Cage's uniform, for example, could remember his father making them for Italian officers during the Second World War: 'I just liked the way he worked with the fabric and understood what our requirements were,' Byrne explains.

What could be purchased in sufficient quantity from Italian dealers were *bustinas*, original Italian army caps, and embroidered badges, including Corelli's cap badge, which is authentic. However, the specific battery-number badges, worn by Corelli and his men, had to be specially made for the film.

Byrne and her team made sure they got every detail right by checking in books and calling on the help of a military researcher Giorgio Cantelli. 'He sourced us originals to look at which we then copied,' she says. 'It is so important to pin down the fine detail.'

Captain Corelli and his men arrive on Cephallonia

Once made, the uniforms needed to look as if they had been well worn and, as time progressed in the film, all the new uniforms had to be put through an ageing process to reflect that. Byrne studied old uniforms to see how this should be done.

'As the wool aged it became flatter and balder and lost its pile. The colour stayed very much the same, but the stitching bleached, changing from the colour of the wool to a bleached-out colour, so we put more fading into it. When you are using new costumes the seams are all bouncy and look new. The breaking down of the new uniforms was a huge process that included sandpapering, spraying with glycerine to mat down the fur, rubbing in Fuller's Earth, spraying in dye, then blow-torching them to take off the pile. It all took a long time, but had to be done otherwise they just wouldn't have looked as if they had been worn.'

The German uniforms were easier to research, but because the Germans on Cephallonia wore thinner, less durable summer uniforms, there was no large-scale stock of them available. In addition, Steven Spielberg's mini-series *The Band of Brothers* and Jean-Jacques Annaud's film *Enemy at the Gates*,

about the siege of Stalingrad, were being shot at the same time and had requisitioned large stocks of Second World War German army uniforms for their projects. As a result, Byrne and her team of seamstresses had to make hundreds of uniforms for the extras who played Germans, and by the end of the twelve-week shoot these were not in great shape.

As with the military clothes, Byrne's inspiration for the civilian clothes, worn by the Cephallonian people, came mainly from studying the photographs collected and collated by art department co-ordinator Rea Apostolides.

'All the Greek islands are different and all the islanders have their own version of what people used to wear and how they wore it,' she says. 'You research it all, but, in the end, you have to find a look that works for the telling of the story in a film that has worldwide distribution and isn't just aimed at Greek islands.'

The work on the civilian clothes began in March in a UK workroom, which comprised two seamstresses and other out-workers; then in April, prior to the beginning of filming, the workroom switched its location to the Athina Hotel in Sami.

As with the military costumes, wherever possible original period clothes were used for the civilians. Many of the garments were hired from costumiers as far afield as Rome, Paris, Berlin and London, but Byrne and her team continued to shy away from using modern copies of period clothes.

The villagers, including Iannis and Pelagia, anxiously await the detonation of a mine on the beach

'With modern makes of period clothes you do not get the look you want to achieve,' she says. 'And whereas a lot of original stock is unusable because it is so faded, old and holed, that was perfect for our purposes. We were also lucky because many costume houses throw out garments in that condition because they think they are too tatty to be worn.'

In the end, a fine balance had to be drawn between using worn clothes and *too* worn clothes. As Byrne explains: 'By the end of the war, the clothes worn by Cephallonians were completely ragged and threadbare, and if we put those on camera it would have looked like joke ageing. You have to know when to draw the line in films.'

When clothes had to be made from scratch, original period fabrics were used, and large quantities of antique linen sheets were bought from Italy and other European cities to make the shirts. Again, these were aged, to make the collar grimy, and to reflect the fact that they were being worn by people who had little money and, therefore, little chance of replacing them.

A man of modest means, Dr Iannis possessed just one suit

Dr Iannis, played by John Hurt, may be rich intellectually, but he is poor financially. He is, after all, serving a community with little wealth and, as we see in the opening scene of the film, is paid with whatever his patients can afford to give him. So throughout the film, Iannis is seen wearing one simple suit. In the movie business, however, nothing is ever quite what it seems – and three seemingly identical suits were made for John Hurt to wear at different stages of the film. The one at the start was padded in accordance with the time of year, and less faded than the one worn towards the end. The changes are subtle, but help to show the passing of time and also, in common with other Cephallonians, Dr Iannis's weight loss due to a wartime lack of food.

Similarly, Pelagia's floral dress seems to change very little during the film, but Penélope Cruz actually wore three slightly different ones. In this instance, the garments were not artificially faded. Instead, the material was printed in three different colour strengths to make each dress appear more sun-bleached than the other. The two 'older' dresses were also sandpapered and patched to reflect how often they had been worn during the years of occupation when no new supplies of clothing could be had from the mainland. Pelagia's slip and bra were also replicas of period versions.

Padding the clothes for scenes at the beginning of the film was kept to a minimum, because as Byrne, who trained as an architect before switching to theatre design and then to costumes, explains, 'It was too hot for too much padding – I'd have had a rebellion.'

However, the costumes for Iannis, Mrs Stamatis and Drosoula were padded so that, as time moved on in story terms, the characters could subtly lose weight to reflect the lack of food on the island.

Above all, Alex Byrne's task was to create costumes which blended with the sets and scenery in which the actors were working. As she says: 'If what we are doing is right, then the audience will believe in the world they are watching and not be distracted by any changes. These should be subliminal.'

The same principle applies to make-up which for *Captain Corelli's Mandolin* was designed by Lois Burwell, who won an Oscar for her work on the Mel Gibson film *Braveheart*, and a nomination for the film *Saving Private Ryan*.

'My job begins when I read the script,' says Burwell. 'I hadn't read Louis de Bernières' book and, after I'd read the script, I decided not to in case it coloured the characters for me.'

Burwell works closely with chief hairdresser Lisa Tomblin, whose previous credits include *Schindler's List* and the James Bond film *Tomorrow Never Dies*. After meeting director John Madden to discuss how he saw the characters, they set about researching the styles and how people would have looked in 1940s Cephallonia.

In keeping with the work of production designer Jim Clay and costume designer Alexandra Byrne, the look that the make-up and hair departments were trying to achieve was to make the cast look as natural as possible with principal cast members, such as Nick Cage as Corelli and Penélope Cruz as Pelagia, blending in with the other actors and supporting artists.

Says Burwell: 'We wanted Pelagia to look young and attractive, but essentially indigenous. We did not want her to stand out like a leading lady – or as a heroine who always looks perfect – because *Corelli* is a company story. Clearly Penélope has a Spanish skin tone, rather than a Greek skin tone, so we needed to make that work on screen. Her skin didn't need to be lightened, but it did need to be modified. Penélope's skin tone borders towards being olive, but it is more of a red than a green olive.'

Tomblin was also determined to achieve a natural look: 'I kept Penélope's hair simple – didn't even brush it, so she has pieces of fly-away hair showing all the time. She's a village girl and I wanted her to blend in with everyone else. Keeping a period feel was important in terms of shaping the hair, while, at the same time, ensuring that the style suited her face. We were very lucky because there didn't seem to have been a specific period look for hair at the time in which the film is set.'

John Hurt, as Iannis, sports a gold tooth in the film – something he agreed to have done, following Lois Burwell's suggestion.

'I thought it added something,' she says. 'It's slightly dapper, characterful and almost eccentric, but not out of keeping with the period.'

A member of La Scala and a prostitute enjoy their day on the beach

Hurt also grew a moustache for the role, and Burwell was delighted with the result. 'Iannis isn't particularly tidy,' says Lisa Tomblin. 'He obviously goes to the barber, but doesn't do his hair every day, just runs his hands through it a lot, so it stands up.'

John Hurt was not the only member of the cast who grew a moustache for his role. 'I asked all the male members of the cast to grow moustaches, and said we'd shave them off if they didn't work,' says Burwell, who was surprised to find that so few of the local men sported facial hair.

According to her, real moustaches made life easier for the actors and extras because 'in forty-degree temperatures it would be necessary to repair fake ones every five minutes when they flapped or sweated off, and this would have been seriously uncomfortable for the chaps concerned'.

Christian Bale, who plays Mandras, could not grow his own beard for his later scenes because the film was being shot out of sequence, and he needed to be clean shaven at other times.

His hair also had to be darkened a little to make his own look more Greek – and when, later in the film, he returns to the island as a partisan, he had to have hair extensions to compensate for the fact that he couldn't grow his own hair because of all the out-of-sequence shooting.

David Morrissey, who plays the German, Captain Weber, is a dark blond in real life. In the film, however, he has to have dark hair because, as Louis de Bernières specifically mentions in the novel, Weber spends as much time as he can on the beach trying to become blonder.

As requested by Burwell and Tomblin, the Italian actors who played the La Scala boys all arrived on Cephallonia sporting long hair and facial hair.

'They all had fantastic but different hair,' Tomblin says. 'It was a great base from which to start work and, after we had given them 1940s haircuts, they soon looked the part. They were very easy to make look good.'

'As requested they hadn't shaved,' says Burwell. 'One of them had a chin beard which he was reluctant to lose, but it went anyway – and another, Sergio, had a great thin moustache which looked so perfect on him we kept it.'

Burwell and Tomblin were at their most active during the crowd scenes, such as the Feast of St Gerasimos, and the German invasion and killing-fields sequences.

'The blood and guts stuff kept us very busy,' says Burwell, whose usual team of six make-up artists doubled to fifteen during the filming. 'The way the schedule was organized meant the German invasion and the Argostoli battle shots were filmed at the beginning of the shoot. For those days, we had all the townspeople's looks to do, plus the entire Italian and German armies – *and* all the principals – *all at once*. It wasn't as if we started by filming two people in the sea; we started absolutely running, the minute we hit the ground.

'Straight after the filming of the battle scenes came the massacre sequence. There was no remission or break while we did relatively simple scenes, such as three people with established looks in a room having a conversation. When you are working long hours and six days a week, the problem is finding the time to work out and co-ordinate what you are going to be doing the following week.'

'Apart from coping with a bit of dust and dirt in the actors' hair, there was much less work for us than for the make-up department during the massacre scene,' says Tomblin.

Burwell agrees: 'That scene kept us particularly busy and there had to be considerable co-ordination between different departments such as make-up and special effects who controlled the squibs [small, aspirin-sized explosive devices which release make-up blood] on the men. The actors were wired to the ground in thick woollen uniforms in forty degrees.'

One member of La Scala – played by Paco Reconti – is given the *coup de grâce* by Weber who shoots him in the head. For this sequence Conor O'Sullivan, a prosthetics expert who worked with Lois Burwell on *Saving Private Ryan*, created a wax layer of skin, beneath which a squib could be placed.

As if the sheer number of people, which the make-up and hair department had to have ready for the battle sequences, was not enough, disciplining some of the Greek conscripts who played Italian and German soldiers was also sometimes a problem.

Mandras as a partisan, looking older and battle-weary

Make-up artists apply special effects blood during the shooting of the massacre scene

'One in ten of the soldiers was supposed to have a moustache, but the young men kept shaving off their facial hair because apparently this is now meant to be a sign of being gay. And, not only did they shave their own moustaches off, when we put on false ones, they'd go to the loo and remove these. So some of them were like naughty schoolboys in this regard, but they liked the blood and guts stuff, apart from the fact that the blood was sticky and attracted flies and bees.'

Tomblin's usual team of five hairdressers was also doubled – and extra barbers were brought in to cut the hair of all the Greek conscripts, local men and stuntmen playing the soldiers. 'Everyone had a hair cut at the start and, for continuity purposes, had to have their hair cut again during the six weeks they were with us,' she says.

In the same way that larger modern bodies had caused headaches for the wardrobe department, the short modern hairstyles favoured by the women who were to play local villagers caused some problems for the hairdressers.

Says Tomblin: 'Although the 1940s style was quite simple – the hair just taken back or young girls wearing it in a couple of plaits – it certainly was not worn short, which was how many of the ladies arrived wearing theirs.'

Tomblin's colleague, hair stylist Ferdinando Merolla, was tasked with the job of arranging wigs or hairpieces for these women and, in the end, most of the extras wore them.

'My biggest headache,' says Lois Burwell, 'was keeping people's skin tones the same from scene to scene. During their days off, people would either go to England, which was covered in cloud and come back pale, or they'd stay on

Cephallonia and either forget the sun block or get burned, and come back darker skinned. We had such a wide variety of skin tones that keeping these within the same range for the sake of the film, so they would not all look peculiar when standing together, was quite a challenge. After all, we had some Greeks in the cast who looked perfect, some Italians playing Italians, some Greeks playing Italians, Penélope, who is Spanish, playing someone who is Greek, John Hurt and Christian Bale, who are British, playing Greeks – and, of course, Nick Cage playing an Italian. To keep everyone in their appropriate grouping and yet true to themselves is one of the hardest things to do because the difference is actually minuscule. At the end of the day, I hope this will be something people won't even think of!'

Polaroid cameras are indispensable to costume, make-up and hair departments, because they enable the teams to check exactly how actors and extras looked the day before or, in some cases, weeks before.

φ φ φ φ φ

Clearly, in a film entitled *Captain Corelli's Mandolin*, music plays an important part. The musical director for the film was Paul Englishby, who trained as a composer at the Royal Academy of Music and has his own jazz band called The Paul Englishby Band. His tasks included teaching Nick Cage to conduct La Scala, arranging the songs the La Scala boys sing, and liaising with composer Stephen Warbeck and mandolin player John Parichelli.

'Nick Cage's singing was fine,' says Englishby, who flew out to meet the actor in Venice one weekend, when Cage was seeing his son, so that he could give the star two hours' training in conducting each day prior to a major scene being shot on the Monday. 'He doesn't have to sing a great deal, but he carries off the bits he does do very well.'

Nicolas Cage rehearses with musical director Paul Englishby

He was amazed at how speedily Cage learned to play the mandolin, and how well he could play it.

'He picked it up *really* quickly,' he says, 'took it everywhere with him and practised all the time. He was only expected to mime, but he could actually play the mandolin, which was fantastic. He's obviously got musical talent, which he never knew he had.'

Englishby's biggest task on the film was arranging music for – and teaching – the La Scala boys.

'I arranged the pieces they sing into a three-part harmony,' he says. 'They were fantastic boys who'd sing all the time on the coach and round the dinner table. They needed to look as if they'd known each other for years and singing was in their bones – and they did. I very much doubt that you'd get ten English actors behaving in that way so naturally, but, in Italy, singing is far more of a way of life.'

John Parichelli, a jazz guitar player who also plays other instruments, had worked with composer Stephen Warbeck before on *Shakespeare in Love*. He had expected that teaching Nick Cage to play the mandolin would be quite a challenge.

'He'd never picked up a guitar or any other stringed instrument before, so – like learning to ride a bike – it seemed a pretty massive task,' he says. 'The original idea was that he would just look as if he was playing, and that it would not be necessary for him to make a sound, but he got it all together and learned to play all the pieces.'

On the screen Cage needed to look as if he was more than just a beginner. As Parichelli explains: 'Corelli is a virtuoso mandolin player, so we had to go into it a bit deeper than just needing a bit of music.'

He expects the film, like the book, to lead to an increase in people wanting to learn how to play the mandolin.

Local people dancing
on the Feast day
of St Gerasimos

'Prior to the book coming out, I think people confused the mandolin with a banjo,' he says, 'but they are very different instruments. A banjo is bigger and basically a cross between a drum and a guitar. Hopefully, the film will increase the mandolin's popularity because it is a beautiful instrument. But even in Italy, where Corelli's style of mandolin comes from, there aren't a massive number of people playing it any more.'

φ φ φ φ φ

Dancing – which includes traditional Cephallonian Greek and the tango – also plays a significant part in the film. Choreographer Quinny Sacks, who was responsible for the ornate Elizabethan dances in *Shakespeare in Love,* was brought in by John Madden to work on *Corelli.*

From the script it was apparent which set pieces she would need to arrange: Pelagia dancing a tango at a party thrown by the Italians, and traditional Greek dances for the Feast of St Gerasimos sequence at the beginning and end of the film, and for Pelagia's and Mandras's betrothal.

Says Sacks: 'My aim – even though one has to break a dance down and teach it to actors who may never have done a particular dance before – was to

make it all look as unchoreographed as possible. At the end of the day, it has to look natural as if it is in their bones. In the 1940s everybody – unlike now – was able to dance. Fortunately, I was blessed with Penélope Cruz who trained as a dancer for fourteen years, which was fantastic. Christian Bale, who had to learn Greek dancing and dance a *mermigas* [a traditional Greek dance] at the betrothal scene, was great too. He has such a facility for learning – has an ease which makes him look very natural. He is an exception to the rule.'

The handsome soldier, with whom Pelagia dances the tango, is played by Nunzio Lombardo, a London-based dancer who helped Sacks as an interpreter and as her assistant when she taught the La Scala boys to dance with the Greek girls who were playing the Italian prostitutes.

'I took one look at the La Scala boys at the airport and thought: "Oh, my God! This is going to be a nightmare,"' she says. 'But they were absolutely delightful, and the rehearsals were a complete giggle and total fun. Fortunately, we were given enough time both to have fun and for them learn how to dance, and they achieved a level of competence. They weren't worried about the steps, they were just being themselves, so when the scene was shot they were completely at ease with the dancing which is an ideal situation.'

Researching the Greek dancing resulted in a few new discoveries for Sacks. 'I did tons of research in England – using books, videos and talking to people who taught Greek dancing – and through contacts in Athens,' she says. 'Ultimately when I got to Cephallonia I threw most of my mainland research out of the window because I discovered that every single island has its own form of dancing, and its own particular dance at a certain time in history.

'I linked up with a girl on Cephallonia who teaches Greek dance and we co-opted some of the locals to come and show us what they did then and what they do now. They were the people who had auditioned – and been chosen – to play Greek villagers in the film, and it seemed only right to see what they could do.'

Sacks says that traditional dancing is still common in Greece, but could be on the wane. 'Sadly, fewer and fewer young men nowadays can do them, but fortunately for our purposes all the young men in the film were supposedly at war.'

φ φ φ φ φ

Voice coach Joan Washington was kept busy on *Captain Corelli's Mandolin* with three different sets of accents and three different nationalities using them. Her work on the film began in October 1999 when she flew to Los Angeles to spend some time working with Nick Cage on his Italian accent. During the next six months, Cage practised at home by listening to tapes; and then, when in Cephallonia, received daily coaching during the two-week rehearsal period.

'Nick was incredibly diligent and kept the accent up pretty much all the time on the set – not in an indulgent way, but just to practise,' says Washington. 'I think it's important not to restrict the practising of an accent to moments when you are acting the part because then you feel as if you are putting on a voice. It was also an incredible help to Nick to be surrounded by the genuine article in the shape of the actors playing the La Scala boys.'

Penélope Cruz may share the fact that she comes from a Mediterranean country with her character, Pelagia, but Washington says that Spanish and Greek accents are very different.

'They may have a lot of sounds in common, but in terms of rhythm and resonance they have nothing at all in common. The Greek accent is about falling and rising, and rising and falling, but the impetus is on the down beat. So that was a challenge for Penélope, because Spanish always tends to be on a rising inflection and is more staccato – like the sound of castanets.'

Like all the cast, Penélope Cruz used tapes in addition to having lessons with Washington. Her Greek stand-in, Despina Ladi, also helped her. 'Everyone worked very hard on their accents and for people like John Hurt and Christian Bale, who were playing Greeks, being on Cephallonia and hearing Greek all the time was very helpful. It's not mimicry, which is something you turn on in order to produce a character, it's organic. John Hurt said something I thought was absolutely right. He thought the accent has to be part of your DNA – not something that is slapped on from the outside.

'Accents – especially Italian accents – are all about sensibility, rhythm, placement and use of language. The Italians relish language in a way that Americans don't. American is very flat, whereas Italian is romantic and melodic.

'Our whole aim for the accents in this movie was that nobody should notice them! There is nothing more boring than a film that becomes a film about people speaking in accents, because then you start listening to the accent and don't listen to the text. So I strive to keep the accents as unobtrusive as possible, with nobody sounding as if they are speaking in broken English. Everybody should sound as if they are speaking in their own language and it should flow.'

φ φ φ φ φ

When a film-maker acquires the rights of a book such as *Captain Corelli's Mandolin*, it is a phenomenal challenge for the production departments. They then need to blend their disparate skills to bring to life what, in this instance, Joseph Heller described as 'a wonderfully hypnotic novel of fabulous scope and iridescent charm'.

And while details, however small, must not be overlooked by actors, make-up, costume, hair and set designers, language coaches, composers and choreographers, and so on, the reality that is created for cinema-goers needs to appear effortless. In film-making, subtlety is just as important as attention to detail.

Chapter 5

EXPLOSIVE ACTION

*'Planes started to hover over us from early in the morning
and the gun emplacements are firing against them. The priest's
wife came and took her belongings. I decided to leave at about
13.00 but the firing became increasingly heavier, as shell-fire
began as well. The shells flew over the house making a horrific
whistling sound. This was followed by the terrifying blast of the
explosion. I locked myself up all afternoon and sat in the dark in
the dining room. I went through real agony.*
*I moved the couch to the office and slept there with my clothes
on, as from 06.00 the large cannons started to fire: the house
trembled as did the glass of the windows and light of the lamp,
which I kept lit throughout the night.'*

Kate Iakovatou-Tool, 15 September 1943

The German troop-carrier cuts through the swell, a few hundred yards off
the shore of the beach. Suddenly there is a roar of shellfire from a nearby
cliff, a brief whistle of a shell flying overhead and then the sea closest to
the craft erupts, spouting waves into the air. It is a near miss. Undamaged, the
ship continues on its way as a Stuka bomber dives screaming towards its gun
position. As the plane releases its bombs with terrifying precision, the Italian
gun and its crew are vaporized.

John Madden's film *Captain Corelli's Mandolin*, set so evocatively against
the stunning background of Cephallonia, does much to bring home the horrors
of war. So realistic are the battle sequences that they stun and set an audience's
hearts racing. For the film-makers, the recreation of these amazing scenes took
months of intricate planning that was worthy of a real-life military operation.
The scale of the battle sequences required the bringing together of every
department involved in the film, so that all of them could co-ordinate their
efforts to produce spectacular scenes.

A German tank breaks
through Italian lines

Director John Madden during the shooting of the action sequences which took weeks to film but take up just minutes of the film

For director John Madden, the battle for Argostoli and the subsequent firing-squad massacre of the Italian soldiers was the dramatic centrepiece of the film. For the millions of people who had read *Captain Corelli's Mandolin*, it would relay the shock and panic that is so vividly described in the novel. And for those who had not read the book, it would be a powerfully moving, unexpected event.

In reality, in the 1940s, the Italians battled with the Germans for ten days. For the purpose of film drama, however, Madden condensed the action into one bloody, awful day.

'The real battle was spontaneous and not terribly well organized. I wanted to portray it as a rude interruption of life in this idyllic world,' he says. 'It was unstable, dirty, chaotic – and catastrophic in its implications.

'It presented certain difficulties for us. There were logistical matters that had to be decided at that point, which if the entire movie had been a war movie would not have been so much of a problem because then all the resources would have been poured into delivering the kind of wattage that is needed for those kinds of scenes.

'The battle sequence itself probably only occupies three minutes of the film's 120-plus minutes, so, in terms of the strategic distribution of resources, it was clear I had to come up with an approach that allowed me to do what was needed without wasting massive amounts of money.

'So the battle was really constructed around the people whose lives we were most interested in – and that was the emotional axis of it. That also meant I didn't have to blow up 5,000 buildings. I only had to blow up one because the action remained with the people whose lives were powerfully affected by what was going on. We set ourselves a limit about the amount of time we could spend on the battle sequence, what we could achieve in that time, and I'm pretty pleased with what we've come up with.

'In the film, the Italians make the fatal mistake of assuming – just as the Italians did in history – that the Allies will come to their aid. Like the true participants, they think all they have to do is to resist the order to hand over their weapons to the Germans. They are vastly in the majority at that point and, given that the Allies are winning the war, they think that history will go their way. What happened, in fact, was that no help came – and Hitler, depending on which source you read, was so incensed that there were German casualties – particularly from a quarter that had only a week or two before been his allies – that he turned on the island and everyone was ruthlessly wiped out.'

For Richard Conway and his team of fourteen special-effects experts, the German invasion scenes took months of preparation. His work began at script stage when he drew up a 'shopping list' of what his department would need to provide – everything from explosions on the battlefield, and bullet hits on Corelli's men as they were massacred by the Germans, to an overflowing well in the village, and a harness for actress Vicki Maragaki when she is 'hung' as Eleni.

And while intricate preparation and planning ahead is vitally important, Conway also had to be flexible enough to be able to deliver anything that John Madden, the director, required. The German invasion and subsequent battle sequences may have been the longest scenes that Conway needed to provide effects for – and certainly the scenes he expected to be the most challenging – but they did not turn out to be the most demanding. That 'honour' was taken by the massacre of the La Scala boys in what was called the killing-fields scene by everyone working on the production.

'I had always assumed that, for this sequence, the shooting would be done with rifles, and I expected around twenty guys to be doing the firing,' he says. 'But it ended up with just two machine guns and twenty people being shot at.'

With the machine guns firing around forty rounds per second, it does not require a mathematical genius to work out that even firing for between three and four seconds at a time takes between 120 and 160 bullet hits – with around six bullets appearing to hit each person. The scene also needed to be shot four times, from different angles, so it became quite an intensive job for the special-effects team.

Every single bullet-hit or squib had to be attached to a back plate and condom that contained the make-up blood, and then be placed on the actor or stuntman and covertly connected by electrical wire to the special-effects team's control box. This meant that the actors and stuntmen playing the La Scala boys had to be rooted to the spot in stifling heat for considerable periods of time, only able to move a distance of two feet in a given direction.

'It was one of the most challenging scenes I've ever done,' says Conway. 'And quite an ordeal because there were an awful lot – about 500 – blood body-hits to make up, together with special harnesses to hide them. And there's a lot involved in making even one work.'

Two of Conway's team spent a month making the bullet-hits. They had to liaise with the costume department because the Italian soldiers' woollen uniforms needed to be weakened in places where the squibs would be placed so that the artificial blood would instantly come through on detonation.

> OCTOBER 1943
>
> *7th Thursday: The sea churns up dead bodies every day. I'm not eating fish any more.*
>
> *26th Tuesday, St Dimitrios Day: I still can't understand how Kefallonia became a front of war: how Argostoli became Italian and Palikin German. And the Italians were about 15,000, well fortified in Livatho with heavy artillery, while the Germans were only 3,000 in the beginning, but due to the passivity of the Italians, they managed to bring another 4,000 élite troops and vanquish them with the assistance of the airforce. People calculate that about 400 stukas were involved in the bombing of the island in different waves. The biggest destruction took place in Farsa, Davgata, Razata, Peratata, and Argostoli.*
>
> EXTRACT FROM DIARY OF KATE IAKOVATOU-TOOL

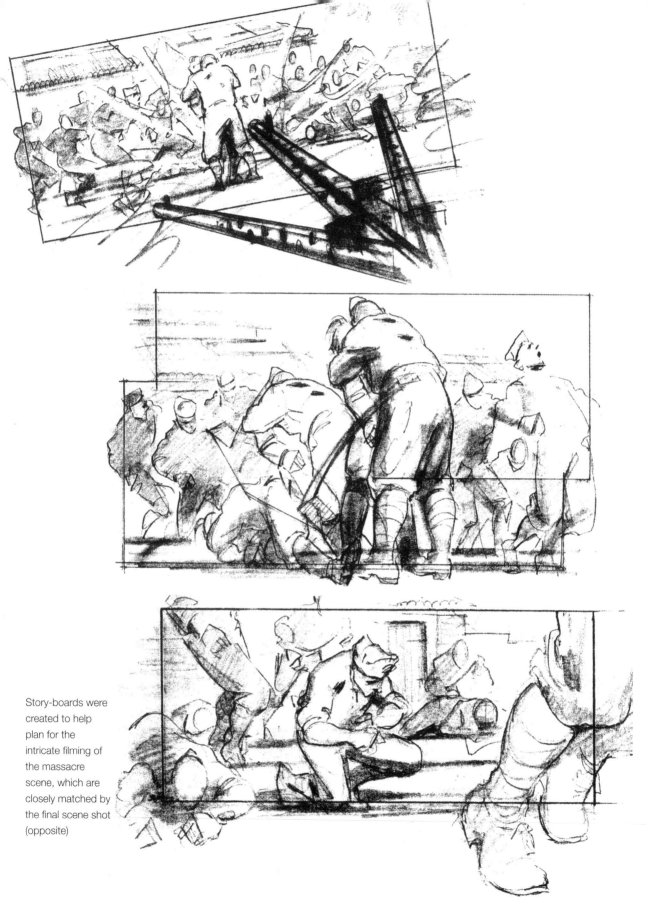

Story-boards were created to help plan for the intricate filming of the massacre scene, which are closely matched by the final scene shot (opposite)

The moment when members of La Scala meet with a sudden and violent end

Different strength squibs were used for the actors and stuntmen. The higher-powered squibs, which pack a punch when detonated, were only used on stuntmen. However, one of the La Scala boys was given a shirt which, by mistake, contained the stronger squib.

'I told him it would give him a "whack", but he was fine about it,' Conway recalls. 'He loved it because, he said, it made him react better. He did actually die bloody well!'

Director John Madden is courteous to everyone and therefore the complete opposite to the image of the archetypal movie director. Despite all the pressures, he remains cool and good tempered. 'Those kinds of sequence,' he says, 'not only require a fantastic amount of thought in terms of how they should be set up, but also logistical planning because they involve wires, resetting times, explosive charges and safety issues. If I had a pound for every minute we spent discussing these things in production meetings, the film would have been in profit while we were still editing it! It was fantastically complicated to do, but hopefully it won't look at all complicated when people watch it.' The firing-squad scene was the one sequence in the film that was story-boarded shot by shot because its vastly complicated nature meant that time would be saved on the day if everything was pre-planned right down to the exact camera positions.

'Frankly, we would have story-boarded the rest of the film, but I'm afraid events bore down on us like a Panzer tank and, time-wise, I had to prioritize what we could and couldn't story-board,' says Madden.

Crew members shield the sun from some of the actors who were connected to the ground by special effects wires and unable to move

'The firing-squad scene was the one that I felt was absolutely essential for all of us to know where we were going and what we were doing, and the assembled sequence is actually very, very close to its story-board. The planning for this was so detailed that even the position of the sun and, therefore, the light played a role in what is possibly the most powerful moment in the film. The precision sharpened – heightened – the drama and showed people's faces with pinpoint detail.'

The fact that they were recreating scenes which had actually taken place on Cephallonia, Madden says, had an impact on them at all times.

'We were constantly struck by the notion – and most particularly while doing the firing-squad scene – that these events *really* had happened; and that men were, in fact, killed all over the island, which is something I can only suggest in the film.'

φ φ φ φ φ

The village of Karavomylos, which was almost completely destroyed by the earthquake and is now totally deserted, was chosen as the site for the killing-fields scenes. While in the village, it is only too easy to let your mind wander and imagine the horrors which first engulfed and then ended in the slaughter of thousands of Italian soldiers – particularly when the film's armourer, Charlie Bodycomb, found a wartime German cartridge case there.

It was something that John Madden felt deeply. 'I was overwhelmed by Karavomylos,' he says. 'It was so very, very redolent with history – and had a

CAPTAIN CORELLI'S MANDOLIN

spooky kind of silence that was terribly powerful. It was exactly the sort of place that the killings would have taken place. And we were aware so much of the time that the fiction we were creating into a film actually overlapped with the reality of people's lives.

'There is an incredible visceral effect that comes from being around a machine gun when it is being fired – of being close to the sheer intensity of vibration in the air and the shattering noise. It really was not hard to imagine what effect seeing and hearing the real thing would have had on those present. It was a *very* disturbing and upsetting scene to shoot.'

φ φ φ φ φ

While – as with all scenes – the safety of the actors and stuntmen was obviously a chief concern during the killing-fields shoot, an extra factor had to be taken into account while filming the German invasion on the beach. When the Italian battery on the cliff opens fire on the German landing craft, explosions had to be seen erupting in the water.

'Because that sequence was to be filmed on Antisamos beach, which is an archaeologically interesting, holiday area with a lot of marine life,' says Richard Conway, 'we foresaw problems about using real explosives in the sea. So we manufactured a compressed air arrangement, which could be floated out to sea, and be made to shoot water eighty to ninety feet into the air.'

The metal structure for this arrangement was made to float just beneath the surface of the water, and any parts that showed during the actual filming were removed, using computer technology, during the editing stage.

The biggest gadget Conway and his team constructed for the film was a fully functional recoil mechanism for the artillery pieces of Corelli's regiment. 'Because the guns were firing level, there was quite a kick-back,' explains Conway. 'They weighed two tons and leapt a foot up into the air.'

The special-effects team studied documentaries and books to see what happened when a 105-millimetre gun is in use.

'When a real shell is fired, there is pressure of around 300 tons that pushes back on the guns,' says Conway. 'We obviously couldn't get anywhere near that, so we manufactured our own lightweight barrel so that we could use much lower pressure and compressed air to make it move.

'Nevertheless our gun still weighed a ton and a half, so – because oil is too slow – we used compressed nitrogen to lift it off the ground when it fired. This meant we were using a pressure of around 3,000 pounds per square inch and, when we released that quickly through a valve, it was virtually an explosive.'

When it came to the shot of the Stuka dive-bombing the Italian gun position – and the gun exploding – real explosives were used. A hole was dug in the rock where the gun was to be positioned and thick, steel metal plates were placed in the hole. The metal plates – known as kicker plates – make sure

A shell lands and explodes in Argostoli – fortunately the debris is actually fake brick made of foam

the explosion will go in the right direction. Sticks of dynamite were then laid on top of the plate and covered with a thin layer of marble dust to hide them.

When Conway electronically detonated the explosives from a safe distance, the area was cleared of all personnel, although sometimes stuntmen would still be in a shot during a smaller explosion. As Conway explains: 'Under controlled circumstances you can use stunt crews, but the Stuka dive-bombing the Italian gun position was going to involve a big explosion.'

Shooting angles were specially chosen so that the gun crew could be seen manning the gun, and then, a fraction of a second later, when the explosion actually takes place, no one will know that the stuntmen were not in the shot.

'That gave us more scope to make the explosion big – and make it like a real bomb exploding,' says Conway. 'In fact, we used about the same amount of explosive that a real explosion would have required – but, of course, without the shrapnel.'

Richard Conway has a British explosives' licence and, once he had been checked out by the Greek authorities, he was allowed to purchase any explosives required for the film. And, understandably, the team's magazine – a large steel container – was kept in a secure place as advised by the Greek police.

The town battle sequences were filmed in Sami and necessitated the partial destruction of Jim Clay's Argostoli set. However, like everything else, this was carefully choreographed and planned. In the film, the town hall comes off worst, following a direct shell hit from a German field gun.

CAPTAIN CORELLI'S MANDOLIN

Before the battle scenes were filmed, the plaster exterior walls of the town hall were replaced by flame-retardant foam.

'This is lightweight and easy to explode,' says Richard Conway. 'It also doesn't travel very far so, to a degree, you can predict where it is going to land. After tests I was able to say where the actors and camera crew could go, but even if it did hit someone it wouldn't really have done any damage.'

φ φ φ φ

While almost everything connected with the film has now been dismantled and removed from Sami, there is a lingering reminder. This is in the shape of a series of tarmac patches situated by the Kastro Hotel on the waterfront road. These now filled-in holes in the tarmac were dug so that the special-effects team could place charges, which would explode when a Stuka – which was added digitally in post-production – is seen strafing an Italian army truck.

'The cannon on a Stuka were quite big, so we had to use something quite beefy in the ground. We used high-grade explosives, placed in tubes in the road, which we then covered with dust to blend in with the road surface,' says Conway.

In the story, the Stuka attack results in the lorry exploding, and, although on the screen it appears to be obliterated, in reality it survived.

Real explosives were used to give scenes maximum visual impact

Corelli and his men approach the Turkish mine found washed up on a beach

'We placed smaller explosive charges all over it, so it seems that the whole thing is wiped out,' says Conway. 'But if we had held the camera on it for longer than we did, you would have been able to see – as the smoke cleared – that it was not destroyed.'

The explosives used on the truck were made from gunpowder, which burns more rapidly than other explosives.

'Gunpowder is a lot more visual, gives off more flame and smoke, and is better to use around people,' says Conway. 'If you use high explosives, you have to use dust and powder because – once it's gone off – there's a big flash and that's about it.'

The shoreline explosion of a Turkish mine alongside Corelli was a challenge for the special-effects team.

'John Madden wanted a really spectacular explosion – including lots of colour and black smoke – on a beach that is listed as one of the most attractive in Europe,' says Conway. 'So we did it in a very environmentally friendly way. The beach is composed of marble cobbles, so we just got hold of two tonnes of marble dust, which is like talcum powder. The mine was made out of fibreglass, and for the black smoke and flame we exploded gasoline, which went straight up into the air with no fall-out.'

John Madden also wanted the sandbag bunker in which Corelli takes cover to be half blown away by the force of the explosion.

'The top half of the bunker was constructed from lightweight sandbags filled with rice husks,' says Conway, 'and at the moment of the explosion we used compressed air to blow the sandbags away.'

Another major challenge for the stunt and special-effects team was to 'blow up' a lorry. This sequence occurs when a German lorry hits a mine during an ambush by Mandras and his partisans. The stuntman inside the truck remained in his seat even during the huge explosion.

Jim Dowdall explains: 'We encased the guy in a kind of cage inside the truck. The cage was made from a material called Macralon, which is basically a type of bullet-proof plastic.'

As ever in such a potentially dangerous sequence, safety precautions were vital. 'He was in a full fire suit, had anti-fire gel on his face and hands, ear plugs because of the blast, and breathing apparatus in case he got enveloped in smoke,' says Dowdall. 'As what we do can never be an exact science, we always overdo the safety precautions. We tested the cage first with no one in it – and it remained intact, with no scorch marks on the inside.'

φ φ φ φ φ

An injured Captain Corelli is carried away following the explosion of the mine

When it came to recruiting the extras to play the Italian and German soldiers, associate producer Susie Tasios once again proved herself to be a resourceful member of the production team. In the many months of pre-production she had been cultivating contacts in the Greek armed forces, in the hope that they could be persuaded to lend manpower and military hardware for use in the film.

'They had never done this before,' says Tasios, a former BBC producer who has lived in Greece for the past twenty-two years and now works as a freelance producer and production manager. 'Unlike countries, such as Ireland for example, Greece hasn't adopted a policy about lending its soldiers to take part in movies.'

The Italians find
themselves surrounded

Nevertheless, in 1998, she began negotiations with the Greek Ministry of Defence in Athens to borrow some men and equipment. Twice her requests were rejected. 'Each time I told them that I was a very persevering person who was never going to take no for an answer,' she laughs. 'As far as I was concerned – and the point I was trying to get over to the Ministry – was that the film was a super project for Greece and that it would probably be the country's number-one marketing tool for international exposure before the 2004 Olympic Games.

'The honour and prestige of giving assistance to a project which would inevitably – given the creative team involved in it – be in line for possible Oscar nominations were things I felt they should take into account. Plus, the long-term economic aspect of the money that would come into Greece on the back of the film, combined with opportunities for Greek technicians to work alongside international film professionals.

'There was an incredible amount of lobbying to do through politicians to persuade the minister of defence and, in turn, the three chiefs of the armed services because there needed to be both political and military approval. It was like handling four completely different sets of negotiations.'

Tasios's perseverance was rewarded. After nearly a year of negotiations, she received some good news. First, the Greek navy agreed to lend two mine-sweepers and crew, then the army caved in and responded with an offer of 107 men. Finally, the Greek air force lent fifty-four recruits. In addition, thirty young local men swelled the ranks.

'The navy was brilliant,' says Tasios. 'It gave us everything free – a complement of ninety-six men, their food, accommodation, even their fuel. Everybody was incredibly helpful. They even shut down their power when we could hear their generators humming during the shooting of the dance scene, and this meant they had no telecommunications for two days. The army, too – once it had agreed – entered into the spirit of it all fantastically well.'

The army recruits camped just seven minutes' walk from the Argostoli set and were given a small allowance by the film-makers.

$$\phi \ \phi \ \phi \ \phi$$

In common with all other aspects of the film, great attention was paid to getting exactly the right type of firearms for every scene.

'Art departments are, quite rightly, fussy and want very specific things, so the role of the armourer is to source the right thing,' says Charlie Bodycomb, armourer on *Captain Corelli's Mandolin*.

And it is not just art departments who notice if a wrong gun is used by a character. As Bodycomb says, audiences increasingly know when something is being used inappropriately.

Captain Weber assures Corelli that he and his men will be safe if they lay down their arms

'If you were to take fifty people at random from the street you would be staggered by their collective knowledge, so it's no good just saying, "No one will notice", because audiences are increasingly historically minded.'

Once he had done a breakdown from the script it became apparent just what a wide range of weapons would be needed for the film:

Argostoli, badly damaged by the battle between Italian and German forces

- Five Beretta 1938A 9mm sub-machine guns (used in the Corelli and Carlo sequences in the Argostoli battle, and by Mandras in the partisan ambush).
- Two Breda mod 1937 8mm machine guns (used by the Italians and the partisans).
- Two Beretta 1934 7.65mm pistols (Corelli's and Pelagia's pistols).
- Forty Mauser K98 carbines (German army infantry rifles).
- Ten Carcano 6.5mm rifles (used by the Italian infantry and the Italian sailors).
- Eighty Carcano 6.5mm carbines (used by the Italian artillery troops).
- Five MP40 9mm sub-machine guns (used by the German infantry).
- Two Luger 9mm pistols (used by Captain Weber).
- Four MG42 7.92mm machine guns (used by the Germans in the execution scene).
- Forty-five miscellaneous guns, including British weapons, used by the partisans.
- Extra fake moulded rubber replicas for the extras to use in long shot, crowd scenes.

'If you are filming something that is set in the twentieth century, then most weapons are readily available,' says Bodycomb. 'The guns used in the *Corelli* film are originals capable of firing, rather than copies or deactivated originals. On some films, though, I find myself working with museum pieces. I don't work very often with deactivated guns because, when the film is being made abroad, you have to do the same paperwork to take a deactivated gun as you do a real gun. So we ship out real ones and the director has the option of firing it or not.'

Researching which guns should be used by each of the protagonists – and then tracking down a source for them – is the part of the job that Bodycomb particularly enjoys.

'I love doing the research, digging around in specialized bookshops, working with the art department and going to museums,' he says. 'It's a bit like detective work.'

Most of the Italian guns came from dealers in America, the German weapons from Germany, but the Derringer pistol, detailed in the script for Pelagia's gun, though not in the end used, was specially acquired at an auction.

Even though the weapons on film sets only ever fire blank ammunition, the guns are real and are, therefore, subject to strict controls.

'You have to get an export licence because they are munitions of war,' Bodycomb explains. 'It can take twelve weeks to get all the papers organized through the British Department of Trade and Industry, and we also have to get the permission of the country in which we are filming. The bigger the presence of stars on the film, the easier that makes it, because they really do open doors.'

All the weapons have to be kept in a secure building with round-the-clock security, as detailed by the local police; and each weapon has to be signed in and out when used.

Even firing blank ammunition, which creates a flash-bang effect but does not fire a projectile, is not without risk. The flash blast could still cause pain if used too close to a body.

'Take an average nine-millimetre calibre pistol,' says Bodycomb. 'Provided your skin is covered by normal clothing when that is fired at your midriff from two or three paces away, you will be fine. But, just the same, you would feel the blast to the chest, which is not pleasant, but perfectly safe.

'In some instances, for the battle of Argostoli sequences, we marked out clear lanes in tape for the soldiers to fire into, because if one of them had dropped the muzzle of his gun into the dirt and dust and got some stones lodged in the muzzle these would have become projectiles which you would not want fired at you. For us, it's safety, safety all the time. It might take a few extra minutes, but that's a small price to pay to avoid someone going off in an ambulance. If we're in any doubt, we test the procedure on paper. We suspend a sheet at what we know to be a safe distance and bring it in a foot at a time. Then, as soon as we get any specking, we know that is going to be uncomfortable.'

φ φ φ φ φ

There is nothing worse than watching a film or television production and seeing the extras, who are playing soldiers, looking as if they have never held a gun before. Fortunately, that is not the case on *Captain Corelli's Mandolin*, because making sure that the men really looked the part was the responsibility of Richard Smedley, a former captain in the British parachute regiment, who has worked as a military technical advisor on films for the past twelve years.

'My job is to ensure that the actual technical abilities – the way weapons are used, the way people salute, march, and the interplay between military figures – are correct,' he explains.

Smedley's research took him to Rome, where he was tutored in Italian military drill by an expert in the Italian army. He also learned the more human side of Italian military life, such as how officers and men behaved towards each other and how the other ranks would treat each other. His research gave the lie to a few popular British historical misconceptions about the Italian armed forces.

'People might think the Italian army is quite informal, but in reality it is not,' says Smedley. 'Those views are based on an inaccurate preconception of the Italian army, and was something I had to rectify for people who were portraying Italian soldiers. In the right situation – such as when it fought the Germans on Cephallonia – the Italian army fought very bravely and had no problem doing so.

'What we have to understand is that the majority of people in the Italian army of 1940 did not have world-domination ideas and did not agree with Mussolini, whom they called "Mussolini the Pig". There is a difference between people who are fighting for something in which they truly believe, or upon which their life depends – and people who are simply ordered to take over a foreign country when really they just want to be at home with their families.'

From Smedley's point of view, the most difficult part of his work on *Captain Corelli's Mandolin* was the sheer number of extras playing soldiers, and the mixture of nationalities.

'Some of the set pieces, such as the disembarkation scenes, were very intricate. And when you've got 150 people present they all have to get it right because it is very obvious when someone is not in step – particularly if he is at the front because then the people behind him are put off as well and it quickly becomes a rag-tag.'

The Greek conscripts, playing Italian soldiers, were given lessons in Italian drill at their base in northern Greece before they arrived on Cephallonia. 'It must have been pretty confusing for them at first,' Smedley says. 'But they came up with the goods.'

On arrival on Cephallonia, all the actors playing soldiers – including Nick Cage – were put through their paces and taught military drill and how to handle weapons and, in the case of those playing Corelli's men, the artillery pieces.

Members of La Scala practise drill

'Like most of the actors, I don't think Nick had done a lot of marching,' says Smedley, 'but he picked it up pretty quickly. It isn't easy. You have to remember that we were teaching people to march in a few days when a real soldier would have had many weeks in which to learn.'

Cage also had to learn how to give commands in Italian and get it right. 'This was not easy either. There's pressure when you have 250 people waiting and wanting to go, and if you get it wrong you've got to go back to the start. But he did fine.'

The British army no longer uses 105-millimetre guns, which were of a similar type to those used by Corelli's regiment, and also the mainstay of most of the world's artillery units since the 1930s. But British arms firms still manufacture them, and Smedley recruited a former British soldier who knew the weapon, as he puts it, 'like the back of his hand'.

'He really made the gun action come into focus and look meaningful,' he adds. 'A real gun crew would have thrown the gun around, rather than just picking it up and placing it, and that's what he did – and encouraged others to do. Little details like that make the action look very real, as did draping people over the barrel to counterbalance it while moving it.'

In one scene, an Italian artillery man is killed by German forces just as he is about to fire the gun. Corelli leaps over one of the field gun's arms and fires it.

'If you are following the textbook, then you wouldn't leap over a gun, you'd go round it,' says Smedley. 'But if you were in action you'd throw yourself over the bloody thing, yank the body out the way, and fire it. Moments like that don't come by textbook, they come from things people have actually seen happen on the battlefield. It's desperate stuff, but it is real.'

φ φ φ φ φ

The action was certainly real enough for one stuntman, who burned his hands while filming the sequence where a Stuka fires its cannon at an Italian truck, which then explodes. Unit nurse Carrie Johnson was on the scene.

'He received second-degree burns, but I don't think there was any nerve damage and he didn't need a skin graft,' she says. 'When the accident happened, we filled an ice-box with water which was already iced, so it was perfect, and put his hands straight into it. As his hands were soaking, you could see that the top layer of the skin was completely black and peeling off straight away.'

It wasn't the only accident that day. Earlier on, another stuntman had been injured while filming a scene with a 105-millimetre artillery piece.

'A gun carriage went over his ankles,' recalls Johnson. 'Brian Bulldock, our paramedic, was convinced he'd fractured both ankles because of the weight of the gun, which we found out afterwards weighed two tonnes and had metal wheels. But the man was very lucky because all the rubble that was lying on the ground must have supported the wheels off his ankles just enough to stop them being fractured. Nevertheless, his ankles were very badly bruised and he was off work for six weeks recovering.'

Fortunately, most of Johnson's work during the filming only involved treating relatively minor injuries. The heat – which reached the mid-forties centigrade at times – was a big problem, despite the fact that she had warned the film unit about the risks before it began work.

'I researched the effects of the heat and sun before I went out to Cephallonia and wrote a paper on it,' she says. 'The idea was for everyone to read it and be able, therefore, to anticipate the problems once they started working in the heat and sun. But I don't think many people bothered to read it.

'So I spent the whole of the first week just running round repeating what I had written. The main point was for people to know about dehydration, and to appreciate the enormous amount of fluids they would need to drink that they wouldn't normally need. At home, we talk about drinking two litres of water a day, but, in somewhere as hot as Cephallonia, that is nothing. At the very least – obviously depending on the size of the person and the activity they are engaged in – people need to drink three times as much. The most I drank in one day was thirty half-litre bottles – I'd started counting because I knew I was drinking a lot.'

In the event, more than 250,000 bottles of water were consumed by the cast and crew during the shooting of the movie.

'The other thing people needed to remember was to cover up. Even though it was May at the start of the filming, the sun was still really strong and we used more than 350 bottles of suntan lotion during the shooting. We didn't always have much shade to begin with, and people needed to break themselves in gently and try to avoid getting burned. We had a few cases of heat exhaustion, but no heatstroke, which is much more serious. That's when you can get brain damage and die. We had the milder version where people feel very lethargic and nauseous, and generally need to take the day off.'

Other ailments that occurred on a regular basis were stomach bugs, sprained ankles, bruises, and aching joints, a common problem among film technicians. As Johnson explains: 'There's just no way to transport a lot of equipment around – particularly things such as big lamps – other than manual lifting. While other industries encourage their staff to use lifting equipment, in the film world everyone is still lifting things manually.'

It is ironic that the action sequences often take many weeks to film but take up only minutes of the final movie. For the film-makers and the cast such sequences are challenging, both physically and emotionally, yet the results on screen are exhilarating. It is knowing that what they are working towards will move and enthral audiences in equal quantities that makes it all worthwhile for those taking part, despite the hardships and sometimes the risks. On *Captain Corelli's Mandolin*, it's clear that their efforts have paid off.

Chapter 6
UNSEEN HANDS

*'I went round to John Madden's house one day to have a
general chat with him and John Parichelli . . . We were all hungry,
so Madden went off to get some sandwiches. While he was gone,
I played a couple of phrases straight out of my head and said to
John Parichelli: "What do you think of that?" He replied: "That's
good." I wrote them down and played a couple more phrases.
'After twenty minutes or so, John Madden came back and
said: "So what about Pelagia's Song?" I said: "Well, I haven't
really worked on it yet, but there is this little piece . . . "
John Parichelli played it on the mandolin and John Madden liked
it. It was actually about two-thirds of the tune that now
exists. But, after our meeting, I went away thinking: "Well, that
can't be any good because I just wrote it while I was waiting
for some sandwiches . . . "'*

Stephen Warbeck, Composer

In a darkened, air-conditioned room of an anonymous office block in a back-street of Sami, film editor Mick Audsley is turning raw film footage shot a few days before, less than two miles away, into something that more closely resembles a movie. There is a common misapprehension that a film editor's work only starts when filming is complete, when they are given canister after canister of uncut footage – 'rushes' – from which they piece together a 'first cut'.

Having an editor on site has two benefits. First, it saves a great deal of time – because if the editing did not begin until the shoot had ended, months would need to be added to the schedule before a film could be released, and this would also lengthen the time before a film could start to recoup some of its costs. Second, being able to see how a film is progressing means that the director, editor and screenwriter can keep a close eye on its development and check whether all the raw material has been shot.

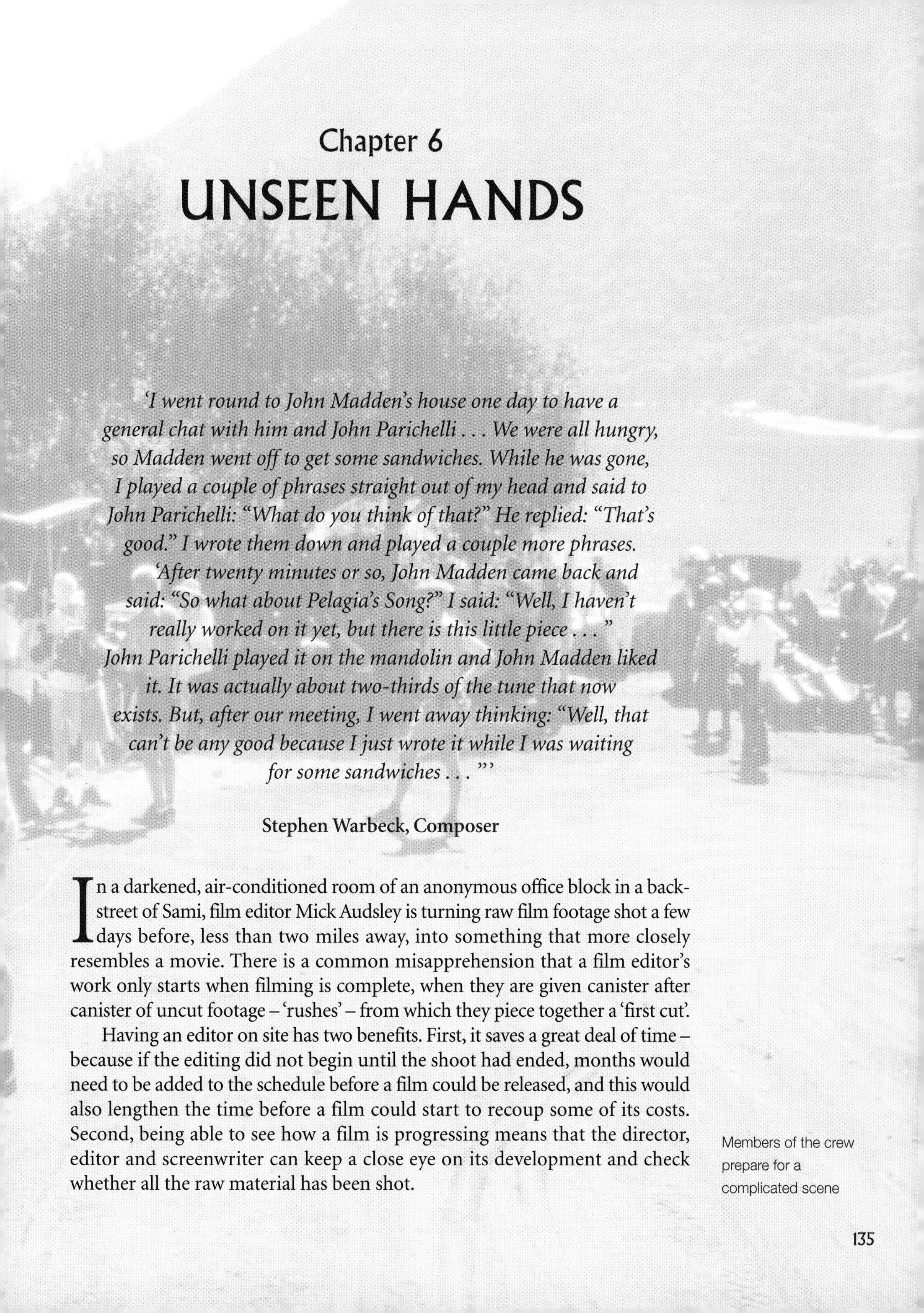

Members of the crew
prepare for a
complicated scene

135

Velisarios (Pedro Sarubi) warns the children to cover their ears before he fires the cannon

Mick Audsley's previous work includes *High Fidelity*, *The Avengers* and *Dangerous Liaisons*. He also helped John Madden with *Shakespeare in Love*. 'The main thing is for me to put the film together, in as sophisticated form as possible, as the footage comes in. Then we have time to respond to what's building up before the other pieces are shot,' he explains. 'This enables us to feel how the film is progressing and if it's speaking in the right voice. It's an exciting process which, in this case, has created a dialogue between myself and Shawn Slovo and John Madden. In many ways, editing is just a continuation of the writing process.

'You are required to be on site because there are always queries to answer about whether things are technically as well as creatively OK, and you need a daily discussion for this which then becomes more fervent as more of the film comes into existence . . . You are also there to sanction when a set can be dismantled, to say: "Yes, this scene is fine – we've got what we want, we're happy." By then, we will have seen a sequence put together in a form, which may not be the final editorial form, but is sufficient for us to know we've got the basic material to make it work. There is always a pressure to take down sets, clear artists – and consequently lower expenditure in that way.'

As is so often the case in the film business, certain scenes had to be re-shot. 'There were a couple of things that had to be redone for focus reasons,' says Audsley. 'These re-shoots were to do with the action taking place in a dark environment, where the lack of light makes filming very tricky. But that's absolutely normal.'

Another reason for some scenes needing to be re-shot was a cacophony of unwanted sounds – both technical and natural: 'There were lots of cicadas crackling away everywhere – and, over a period of a few weeks, they seemed to get louder and louder. Some lights also have a tendency to hum which is then picked up on the sound recording.'

φ φ φ φ φ

The newly shot film for *Captain Corelli's Mandolin* was sent back to London on a daily basis by a rushes runner, a member of the crew hired specifically for this task. Usually travelling on a direct charter holiday flight, the canisters of film would be placed in the hold of the plane like any other piece of luggage.

Back in London the following day, the film would be processed, printed and checked, then a report given to Mick Audsley or one of his two assistant editors, Mags Arnold or Aggela Despotidou. Staff in the production company's London cutting rooms would then synchronize the sound and the pictures before sending it back to Cephallonia, again by courier.

After long days spent shooting, John Madden, Mick Audsley and other members of the unit would then travel to Aghia Efimia, to sit in a small hall and

An anxious Pelagia wanders through Argostoli in the aftermath of the German invasion

Pelagia and Lemoni
in the town square,
listening to Corelli
play his mandolin

watch the footage. A copy of the footage – made on videotape – would then be fed into a powerful editing computer for Audsley to start the editing.

'Until relatively recently – maybe four or five years ago – I physically cut the print, and joined and made the reel myself,' says Audsley. 'But the speed, variation and sophistication that can now be achieved is so much quicker with what I call visual word-processing.'

Typically, Audsley would have been editing footage filmed just four days previously. 'I tried to keep up behind them – something that would have been impossible in the days when I was physically cutting the print. The new technology has really halved the time it takes to assemble the film. What, once upon a time, would have taken me all day, I can now do by lunchtime.'

All this meant that by mid-September 2000 – just two weeks after finishing shooting – John Madden and key executives were able to see what is known as the 'writer's cut'. 'This is the first cut – the result of all the shooting and editing. It is called the "writer's cut" because we are putting on the screen everything that was written – and shot. After that, we whittle away and comb through it all again to see how efficiently and most interestingly we can make the story work.'

For the next month Madden and Audsley were locked away in an editing suite at a post-production house in London, so that Madden could make the final decisions about exactly how the film should look for its test screenings in late October.

φ φ φ φ

The reasons why millions of readers adored Louis de Bernières' novel *Captain Corelli's Mandolin* – its vast tapestry, vivacity and ease with which it flits from one character to another – were among the same reasons why it was such a challenge for screenwriter Shawn Slovo to adapt the book for the big screen. She knew it would be a tough assignment the moment she accepted the job, but she also relished the marvellous opportunity to work on such a fascinating text.

'I thought it was going to be a *very* difficult task,' she admits, 'because it's a very rich book which, in dramatic terms, has big problems from the point of view of adaptation simply because it is so rich, and sprawling, and huge, and flicks from story to story, whereas a film needs to have a much tighter dramatic structure. It was certainly going to need a lot of reinvention and reworking.'

At the beginning, while working with Roger Michell, Shawn began the obvious but none the less difficult task of deciding what to leave out of the film.

'We started in a very mundane way crossing out what we didn't think was going to work. Then I rewrote the story, because – before I started writing the script – I wanted to tell the story in a long-hand version. We worked on that. Then, finally, when we were happy-*ish* I started writing the script.'

As, in between these sessions, Michell and Slovo were also working on other projects, the script-development process continued for several years.

'I would do a block of work on it and then go off and do something else. Then, when Roger was available, we would revisit the script and I'd do another draft,' Slovo explains. 'So I mainly wrote drafts during that period because it was such a protracted development process.'

With every new draft came alterations: new sections added, other sections excluded.

'Things kept changing,' says Slovo. 'It becomes a very dynamic process that began to take on a life of its own. Some things don't work, and you come up against problems of drama and character, so you keep reinventing in order to address that. It changes all the time. It's a very fluid process.'

Mandras prepares to throw Pelagia playfully into the sea

What never changed, however, was Slovo's assessment of the central emotional core of the novel – and hence the film. 'The hook was the love story because that's what gives people access to the story and the characters,' she says. 'It's what readers respond to – and what cinema audiences will respond to.'

Although the love story is the key theme in the film, Slovo says that most of the major changes that were made when adapting the book to the film script were in that central story.

'In the novel, the character of Captain Corelli does not really change from the beginning to the end,' says Slovo. 'He remains the same man, which is not the stuff of film drama. So that's where the fundamental changes were made and these obviously had an effect on the love story.'

The book, which is both very funny and profoundly moving, sometimes at the same time, begins with a highly amusing scene involving Dr Iannis, and a man called Stamatis, and a spherical object – a pea – which, unknown to everybody, had lodged in Stamatis's ear in childhood and caused him to be deaf in that orifice ever since.

Slovo decided that the film should start in the same way. 'It's a very amusing

Corelli and Pelagia say their goodbyes before the fighting begins

sequence and sets the tone for the film. It instantly portrays an unusual world, which is very European, original and non-generic, and I think that's part of what charms the readers, and will hopefully charm the film audience without being too flaky. I think it's an absolutely wonderful way to open the film.'

One person who did not figure large in Slovo's conversation about the structure of the film was Louis de Bernières, the author of *Captain Corelli's Mandolin*. 'I met him just once, but we had no conversation at all about the scripts,' says Slovo. 'We have had conversations since and, as you would expect, he has ideas and views about the script. But once you have sold your novel, you've let it go really, and don't have much choice. If you want to keep control, then you don't sell it, or you write the script yourself, or produce the film yourself, and Louis is not a screenwriter just as I am not a novelist, so it's a different area.'

Large-scale Hollywood films are often in development for many years and, before they are finally finished, have often worked their way through countless actors, directors and whole teams of screenwriters. The change of director on *Captain Corelli's Mandolin* obviously had a massive effect but, that aside, little else, in terms of the cast and writer, altered during the development process. This is something that Shawn Slovo is pleased about, because many writers are swept off a project when a new director becomes attached to it.

'I'm very proud,' she smiles. 'I want a T-shirt saying: "I've survived the transition of directors", because there was a wobbly moment when we were having difficulty with the script, when we just didn't have enough time, and when there was, as a result, talk of bringing in someone else who would have a fresh approach that might be able to speed things up. A studio's solution is usually to get another writer. It's just a knee-jerk reaction – but *here I am*!'

Dr Iannis with Stamatis (Gerasimos Skiadaresis) and Mrs Stamatis (Aspasia Kralli) in the film's opening scene

There is an irony in the fact that the relatively short period of time available before the film went into production, necessitated – enabled – Shawn to be on set in order to have a constant dialogue with director John Madden and editor Mick Audsley, and to rework certain sections of the script as the film was being shot. This meant that the constant communication between the trio – as well as other members of the production team and cast members – gave extra collaborative opportunities and helped the organic feel of the production.

'It doesn't always happen that the scriptwriter is on the set,' says Slovo. 'And the fact that I was is much to do with the kind of man John Madden is. He's very secure and stable, and doesn't feel threatened by the presence of the writer. Also, I totally understand that, while a film is a collaborative process, once the shooting starts it is the director's thing and the main brunt of the scriptwriter's work has been done. When the film moved into John's arena, I was completely respectful of that and trusted him completely.

'I think writers should be on the set to deal with all kinds of things, such as production problems, that crop up and to keep an eye on how things are going and the knock-on effect this may have on other sequences that are coming up. But the main reason I was on set was that we had so little time.

'Even during the filming we still had scenes that were not properly "landed", and I was working on these with John in Cephallonia. I would write them, he'd rewrite them, I'd rewrite, and then he'd give me his notes and I'd rewrite again . . . '

This process could, of course, have taken place by fax or e-mail, but nothing beats the opportunity to talk about a scene – or a section of dialogue – face to face; and it also meant that Madden and Slovo could watch the rushes every day and discuss what had been captured on screen.

'Ideas and views come up when you see the rushes and you may suddenly think: "Actually, we don't need this particular bit", or "This is wrong", or "We're going to have to rewrite this to compensate for that".'

φ φ φ φ φ

Back in London, the film-score composer, Stephen Warbeck, who had won an Oscar for his work on *Shakespeare in Love,* had already composed two key pieces of music for the film – a tango, which Pelagia dances with a handsome Italian soldier, and what is known as 'Pelagia's Song' – before shooting even began.

Pelagia's Song is a beautiful piece, which we could be forgiven for believing that Warbeck laboured over for many weeks. Surprisingly, though, he says this was not the case.

'I went round to John Madden's house one day to have a general chat with him and John Parichelli,' he recalls. 'I'd just played "Santa Lucia" or something because John wanted to hear it to decide whether it was a good idea for one of

CAPTAIN CORELLI'S MANDOLIN

the songs that the La Scala boys sing. We were all hungry, so John went off to get some sandwiches. While he was gone, I played a couple of phrases straight out of my head and said to John Parichelli: "What do you think of that?" He replied: "That's good." I wrote them down and played a couple more phrases.

'After twenty minutes or so, John Madden came back and said: "So what about Pelagia's Song?" I said: "Well, I haven't really worked on it yet, but there is this little piece . . . " John Parichelli played it on the mandolin and John Madden liked it. It was actually about two-thirds of the tune that now exists. But, after our meeting, I went away thinking: "Well, that can't be any good because I just wrote it while I was waiting for some sandwiches . . . " And so I wrote three or four more possible Pelagia tunes.

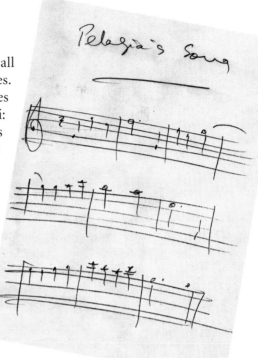

'A short while later, I went back to John and played these, but we didn't like any of them nearly as much as the first. They were all fine, but there was something so right and appropriate about the first one that we chose that.'

Much of Stephen's inspiration for the song came from reading de Bernières' novel. 'I think the ease with which the song came is a testament to the power of the book and the script, and the conversations I had with John about how Corelli's and Pelagia's relationship was going to be. When reading the book, I had a very strong feeling about their relationship. I cared a lot about both of them – just as I do now when seeing the film – and that makes it so much easier to write a tune. If you don't really care about the characters – don't respond to anything about them – it's devilish.'

Writing for the mandolin was also a pleasure for Warbeck. 'I *love* the mandolin and have three of them,' he says. 'Whenever I went to Greece on holiday I took one with me – so me, Greece and the mandolin happened a long time before I read the book. In fact, I probably wouldn't take a mandolin to Greece now because I'd be too self-conscious!'

In addition to reading the book, the script and talking to Madden, Warbeck also spent some time researching Italian and Greek music to give him inspiration.

'It's just part of the preparation you do,' he said. 'It's the thinking about Pelagia and Corelli, the listening to tapes of Italian mandolin music, Greek music and popular Neapolitan songs – all that kind of stuff bubbling away even while you are washing-up or doing other mundane things . . . Without being precious about it, tunes kind of create themselves all the time, so when you actually write them down it doesn't necessarily take very long.'

Writing scores for films, however, can be – as Warbeck explains -a painful process: 'I remember when I was on *Mrs Brown* having a bottle of wine and listening to a lot of Mahler one evening, and thinking: "I'm never going to be able to do this . . ." Then I'd go off to do something like trying to mend a bicycle pedal and then – having taken that constructive diversionary tactic – come back in a more positive mood, quite eager to work. The nearer it gets to your deadline, the less you can wait for the right frame of mind!'

Sunday, 3 October, was the date set for the first recording of the provisional soundtrack for *Captain Corelli's Mandolin* with a fifty-piece orchestra, including a fully orchestrated version of Pelagia's Song. That session was then followed by further recordings with a seventy-piece orchestra, which features on the soundtrack and the album.

'People criticize films for being manipulative, and that can be very tricky because, in a way, music is manipulative. It *can* make you feel differently about something – otherwise, what's the point in having it there? So it is designed to change the way people think or feel about something.

'I suppose the music composer's job is to unify a film – to find ways to reflect certain parts, the anxieties and passions, and to sew the film together. So, if the action involves a great love or a great loss, the great loss can be felt in the

Corelli and Pelagia are reunited

CAPTAIN CORELLI'S MANDOLIN

great love, and the great love in the great loss . . . Musically, you can draw the audience's attention to those links and also make links that they wouldn't necessarily have been aware of.'

Warbeck – who began playing the piano at the age of four, who once dreamed of being a rock musician and has a band called The Kippers – agrees that film music should not be intrusive, but should blend with the visual imagery.

'It does depend on the film and how much music there is,' he says, 'but I'd say there are an awful lot of times where the music could, but shouldn't be noticed – like your head and shoulders shouldn't be sticking up above the wall.'

In addition to working with John Madden on *Shakespeare in Love* and *Mrs Brown*, Warbeck also worked with the director on *Prime Suspect IV* and *Truth or Dare* for television.

'One of the many things that is impressive about John is his tremendous musical memory,' says Warbeck. 'I play a group of themes or cues on the piano and he is able to refer back to one I'd played a couple of hours ago, and say: "That theme you played when I first came in – the one that was bit like this – try that here . . . " He sort of shelves them as he hears them, and then often remembers them better than I do because I have them written on a bit of paper whereas he's just listening to them.

'More importantly, some of his instincts and mine, about what we want the music to do for a picture, coincide. Neither of us particularly appreciates music that answers the question – we like the music to leave the question unanswered. So if you have a love scene and go absolutely flat-out with that, it's like closing the door and saying: "There it is . . . That's that sewn up . . . She's in love with him . . . end of story." Whereas music can pose or leave a question – suggest a danger – ask does she *really* love him? In *Corelli*, the question is, is Pelagia in love with Mandras?

The full orchestrated score for Pelagia's Song

'I think John and I both respond to that level of musical contribution rather than the toothpaste-style advertisement where you say: "What a beautiful place, what a beautiful romance, here we go . . . " In the *Corelli* film, there's always a running against everything. There is obviously a tension – the war continues almost throughout the whole film – so there are strata which run in different ways to counter the stratum above – and the music can help, can unsettle or excite you, or can do things that the picture isn't necessarily doing. It adds another dimension.'

In the same way that the work of other departments blends effortlessly to create a vivid and real picture on screen, the roles of the unseen hands should never be overlooked. The efforts of the editor, the screenwriter and the composer are vital to the process of film-making, even if to some their jobs lack the glamour of those of other members of the production team. Their work is almost subliminal, but movie-making is a collaborative process, and what they add to a film is vitally important and really makes a difference.

Mandras, before war turns his life upside down

Chapter 7

A CAST OF CHARACTERS

'It is incredible that so few know about the massacre on Cephallonia. We are talking about the murder of 10,000 people on quite a small island . . . And the scariest thing is that nobody helped them: the Americans didn't, the Italians didn't, and the English didn't. It was just a strange almost surreal incident, and I am happy to be a part of the telling of their story.'

Nicolas Cage

Finding the perfect cast for a film or play is part guess-work, part hunch and part luck – all combined with the experience and instincts of the director and the casting director. Another key consideration, though, is box-office 'draw' and 'fire-power', and in the case of *Captain Corelli's Mandolin* securing an A-list Hollywood star, such as Nicolas Cage, is enough to have film company bosses feeling much more relaxed about putting their hands into their pockets to bank-roll a movie. The addition of other proven favourites, such as John Hurt and Christian Bale, and exciting fresh talent – at least outside Spain – such as Penélope Cruz, all serve to boost the feeling that the film is rather special.

But it is not just the casting of the lead roles that requires great care and attention. An epic film relies just as much on the calibre of its supporting cast members. Based in London – and working with counterparts in Athens and Rome – casting director Mary Selway assembled some of Europe's leading character actors to play the smaller, but none the less vital roles.

Then for La Scala, dozens of Italian actors were interviewed and shortlisted by Selway and then chosen by John Madden. On Cephallonia the young Italians, most of whom had never met before, bonded and really became La Scala, off set as well as on. Like the characters they portrayed, they would sing at almost any opportunity and with their natural exuberance and love of life, they helped to bond the rest of the cast together. As a result, there were no boundaries between cast and crew – be they American, English, Greek or Italian – and the spirit of enthusiasm helped to enhance and bring more magic to what is now seen on the screen.

Nicolas Cage as Captain Antonio Corelli

Never let it be said that Nicolas Cage does not enjoy a challenge – because his role in *Captain Corelli's Mandolin* was certainly that. Far from simply requiring acting skills, the part also called on him to learn a diverse set of skills. These included speaking with an authentic Italian accent, in a wide range of circumstances from commanding the men of an artillery unit to tender love scenes with Pelagia, marching, drilling and looking as if he had been in the army for years, singing opera arias as if he had known every word and nuance since childhood, plus the need to look as if he is a virtuoso on the mandolin.

These requirements presented unique challenges – and an unusual start to working on the production. For the first three weeks on Cephallonia instead of attending rehearsals, Nick found himself on a steep learning curve.

'As soon as I arrived I found myself in the thick of it,' he laughs. 'From ten to twelve in the morning I would have dialect and accent lessons, from one to four military training, from five to seven script read-throughs, and from seven to eight mandolin lessons.'

From the moment he read the script, however, Nick was enthralled by the idea of being in *Captain Corelli's Mandolin.* 'I read it at a time when I was feeling very emotional about love, love stories and romantic situations, and it *really* spoke to me. I thought it was a tremendous love story – and I have always been partial to romantic prose.'

Nick was first brought aboard the project when Roger Michell was the film's director; and, when John Madden took over from Michell, Nick anticipated that *Captain Corelli's Mandolin* would be a very different film. 'The movie we have made now is entirely different from the movie I originally said yes to. When Roger had to withdraw and John Madden came on board, I was very excited to work with him, but when I read the new script it was, as I had anticipated, very different. It definitely involved an adjustment for me – not because I was in any way frightened by the material, but because I had to rethink it and re-understand the character of the person I was to play. What Madden did was to introduce a lot more of the realistic effects of war into the love story, which meant that I could access more emotion for the part of Corelli. Madden made the film less pretty, and perhaps more authentic.'

The character of Antonio Corelli was also a considerable draw for Nick.

'Corelli is unlike anyone I have played before,' he says. 'When we first meet him he is truly a *bon vivant* – a man who lives for the moment, enjoys life to the full and really celebrates being alive. But his experiences then are only half complete. He is not fully aware that there are other forces in the world, such as war, that can't be denied. To begin with, his time on Cephallonia is really like a holiday. He's there, playing his mandolin, and his men are all singing opera, drinking wine and flirting with prostitutes.

(Opposite) Captain Corelli recovering from his injuries after the massacre

'Meanwhile, the Greek partisans are battling with the Germans, to try to keep their country. At first, Corelli is blind to all this, but then the tragedy happens to him and his men – a wake-up call from hell – which opens his eyes and he becomes a different person, a ghost of the man he once was, and doesn't want to play mandolin any more. I think the idea is that through this experience he can grow, can become an even better version of his old self.'

The fact that the massacre of thousands of unarmed Italian soldiers, fictionalized in the book, really took place – and that, nearly six decades since the end of the Second World War – it remains a relatively unknown event, even in Italy, shocked Nick Cage.

'It is incredible that so few know about the massacre on Cephallonia,' he says. 'We are talking about the murder of 10,000 people on quite a small island … And the scariest thing is that nobody helped them: the Americans didn't, the Italians didn't, and the English didn't. It was just a strange almost surreal incident, and I am happy to be a part of the telling of their story.

'Cephallonia is known to have a curse that gives you bad dreams and, interestingly, a lot of the crew had horrible dreams – some of them violent nightmares. Even in the script, it says that the island has been steeped in blood,

Captain Corelli playfully swings Lemoni in the doctor's garden, much to Pelagia's annoyance

A relaxed Corelli
conducts members of
La Scala

massacres and slaughter for 1,000 years – and I can't help but think that, somehow through the metaphysical side of our self, these vibrations – souls – seep into our brains while we sleep. I feel like I am supposed to tell this story, and that maybe these energies – or whatever else we would call them – are still there in some way.

'The movie focuses quite a bit on the agony of the massacre of Corelli's men in the firing-squad incident – and culminates in that horrifyingly shocking moment. It is impossible for me not to feel I am in touch with ghosts in Cephallonia. I never thought they would hurt me, though, because I felt they wanted me to tell their story.

'I had some really bad dreams. They were always violent, and involved soldiers and killing. The worst one was where two soldiers were stabbing each other in the face with knives and bayonets. It was very real and bloody, and woke me up. In a way, dreams are like gifts when you are acting because you can retain the feeling of the dream – the horror of it – and put that into your work. In this instance, it meant I could recall it when I was being filmed in the firing-squad scene – the sequence when Corelli sees all his men massacred.'

It was clearly an authenticity requirement that Nick Cage should be totally believable when, as Antonio Corelli, he plays the mandolin.

'This was something that worried me,' he admits. 'I was very daunted by the challenge because I'd never played a musical instrument before. As a child I'd tried to learn both the piano and the clarinet, but to no avail. I bought a mandolin even before I started work on the film and had a couple of lessons. Then, when I arrived in Cephallonia, I started working with Paul Englishby and John Parichelli, and they gave me a CD and showed me how to hit some notes and chords, and I just went over it all, time and time again.

'This went on and on until, about three weeks into the rehearsing, I started to feel comfortable with it. But the mandolin didn't really come together for me until about a month into the shooting. The secret is to put in the hours – and, for me, the time was about an hour a day every day – and then, throughout the day, just pick the instrument up, and go through the songs when you have a few minutes until you make it look like it's easy.'

There is no trick photography in *Captain Corelli's Mandolin*, and Nick won considerable plaudits from the film's musical advisors for his dedication to playing the mandolin. His musical proficiency, gained in such a short space of time, also gave director John Madden a wider choice of camera angles.

'The hardest moment,' Nick says, 'was the sequence when Corelli is playing Pelagia's Song in public for the first time. For this, the camera is on me, wandering down to my fingers and then coming back up, so you see me playing without a cut. *And* I wasn't playing against a playback of John Parichelli's playing. I had to play it live. I was wearing Corelli's thick woollen uniform for that scene and was sweating a bit I can tell you!'

Nick was also keen that his conducting should look realistic as he is the nephew of conductor Anton Coppola and the grandson of Carmine Coppola, the conductor and composer whose credits include the music for *The Godfather* films. 'It was intimidating because the conducting had to look good and there are a lot of people out there who are very keen on music and who know what conducting is. I didn't want them to say, well that was bull****.

'The fact that my late grandfather was a conductor really anchored me. I felt I could do it because it was in me somewhere. So when I did the conducting on the beach I was nervous and would think: "Here we go, the camera is rolling and now it's time"– and then I would just say: "OK, Grandpa, you're going to be there with me – let's do this!"And I would psyche up that way.'

This may have been hard work at the time, but Nick considers it all to be part of the job. 'One of the reasons why I decided to become an actor was I didn't really know what I wanted to be, and knew that the research process involved in acting would enable me to learn a little about everything. So, because I take my acting seriously, it forces me to really concentrate and try to learn something. And I'm glad I did in this film because the mandolin, like the piano and clarinet that I tried to learn as a kid, was probably something I would not have stuck with if I hadn't had to. Now it is something I wouldn't mind continuing to work with.'

Even more difficult than learning to play the mandolin was learning Italian army drill skills – and the marching.

'Those were probably the least fun things I got to do on the movie,' Nick admits. 'Learning how to shout orders and march – and take orders – was quite an experience . . . It's like taking a vacation from yourself because – as a soldier –

you are not allowed to think, you just do what you are told. This might be beneficial in some cases – not just for actors but for anybody whose life doesn't have much structure – because you are freed from your own issues. But, as a rule, the military experience is not a lot of fun.'

As Captain Corelli, Nick also had to look as if he was more competent than his men.

'I had to march really well – and learning to shout orders in Italian was another challenge. I also had to arm a cannon in Italian, and the La Scala boys and I had to get together with Richard to go through all this. After a couple of weeks, it started to fall into place. But I wasn't as skilled as the rest of La Scala because they were doing it on a daily basis while I was at rehearsals, having dialect lessons, and doing all kinds of other things – but everyone seemed to be happy with the results.'

Although Nick's roots are Italian, he does not speak the language.

'I need to learn it,' he smiles. 'It's a language I know I would enjoy. On the movie, I spent a lot of time with Italians and went to Italy at weekends to spend time with my family, and to get the flavour and sense of the place. I *really* love it. The Italian language is very melodic – certainly more so than English which can sometimes sound very harsh and doesn't flow as much.'

While on Cephallonia, Nick was able to spend time with his friend John Hurt, whom he has known for some years.

'John is great,' he says. 'He's a master – and I've been a fan of his for years. He's a very fine gentleman, so when I found out he was also in the film I was thrilled because I had been trying to work with him for a long time.'

Nick was also impressed by Penélope Cruz – who plays the woman his character is in love with in the film.

'Penélope has become a friend. I'd seen some of her work, including *All About My Mother*, before we acted together,' he says. 'She's *really* great in *Captain Corelli's Mandolin* – her acting is very raw and instinctive. She has a tremendous emotional capability, and is quite electric on film.'

Nick, who is acknowledged as one of Hollywood's most versatile actors, and is equally well known for his poignant portrayals in dramas and comedies, such as *Birdy, Moonstruck, Honeymoon in Vegas, It Could Happen to You, Leaving Las Vegas* (for which he won a Best Actor Oscar), *Face/Off, City of Angels, Bringing Out the Dead* and *Gone in 60 Seconds*, also enjoyed working with director John Madden.

'He is an incredibly pleasant man – and I never once heard him raise his voice or saw him lose his cool,' he says. 'He gets the job done as good as anyone else without needing to do either of these things, and so commands respect.'

Penélope Cruz as Pelagia

Penélope Cruz was certainly moved by the raw emotion of *Captain Corelli's Mandolin* from the very first moment she read the script.

'I read it on a plane while travelling from Los Angeles to London, and, as I got further into it, started to cry and pray I'd get the part of Pelagia,' she recalls. 'I was amazed by the story and the characters, and it really touched my heart. I knew that I really wanted to do it and was ready to fight for the part.'

She met director John Madden, first in London, where she read some scenes, then in Los Angeles, where she was filming the movie *Blow* with Johnny Depp. A few days later, she says, Madden telephoned her with some good news.

'John said: "Some parts belong to certain people and this one belongs to you." I was *very* happy – *very* excited.

'The film is really about love,' she says, 'and the way I see it is that there are three different Pelagia love stories: the one between father and daughter, the one between Pelagia and Mandras, and the relationship she then has with the love of her life, Antonio Corelli.'

What interests Penélope in playing the role of Pelagia is the journey that her character embarks upon.

'Pelagia goes through so much,' she says. 'The story begins with her as a young girl who hasn't had much experience of life because she has spent much of her time studying with her father. But, as time goes on, so many things happen to her that she becomes, not exactly a completely different woman but a person who, in losing some of her past, gains so much from the pain of what she goes through. She's not a victim – she's a fighter who accepts that these events are part of life.

'I *really* like her. She's intelligent, not only because she's intellectually prepared by her father, but also because she has common sense and respect for people. She is preparing to become a doctor, speaks several languages and, despite her youth, is wise, which must come from her relationship with her father, who is a great man.'

The life of everyone on Cephallonia is, of course, disrupted by the Italian invasion, but Pelagia's world is particularly altered the moment she and Corelli see each other as he leads his men into Argostoli.

'She likes him from the first moment she sees him, but also knows he means trouble,' says Penélope. 'She knows this is something she must face because, as their relationship develops, what she feels for him is bigger than anything else. Even when she gets angry with him – such as when she asks him how it is possible for him to enjoy himself with his men and their prostitutes on the beach in the middle of a war – she also values him for being like that. At the same time, she knows she is falling in love with him and that maybe she should not be, but love is not something that can be planned.

'I think Pelagia has the feeling we have sometimes, when meeting someone, of feeling that we know the person from somewhere before – maybe from another life. I think she and Corelli immediately *feel* something for each other, that this is something Pelagia doesn't want to admit to but, at the same time, cannot hide.'

Pelagia's feelings for Corelli leave her unsure about how she feels for her first boyfriend, Mandras. 'He's her first love, they have a good time together, and there is a lot of desire between them,' says Penélope. 'But their relationship hasn't really had time to grow and develop. At the same time, I think Pelagia has perhaps realized that their relationship might not work but doesn't really want to admit this to herself or to Mandras.'

On the first day of filming Penélope found herself quite literally in at the deep end, when she was filmed in a scene in which Mandras playfully throws Pelagia into the sea from a small wooden jetty.

'That actually was a good way to start,' she smiles, 'because, during the first few days of a film, I always feel as if I have never made a movie in my life. I feel new to the whole thing, which is actually good because it is dangerous to get into thinking you know how to do this job because, in reality, you do not. Of course, it gets easier, but you never quite lose the sense of fear and insecurity, and this is what keeps you on your toes.'

Pelagia returns with her basket having gathered medicinal herbs

In *Captain Corelli's Mandolin* Penélope has to work with three leading men, Nick Cage, Christian Bale and John Hurt. 'All three are very different, but special men,' she says. 'Christian is very funny, John is charming – and I was amazed by Nick. I've always admired his work, but what he has achieved in this movie is incredible. There is so much heart in his performance. He is someone who was born for the job he does – it's in his blood – and he's so full of life. His self-control in relation to his acting is amazing.'

Penélope was able to demonstrate her own skills as an accomplished dancer in the film. 'I began dancing when I was four and studied ballet for fourteen years. It was great to be able to dance in the film because I do miss dancing,' she says. 'I had to dance the tango, which is a simple dance, but then it didn't need to be a really impressive dancing display because this sequence comes at a moment when Pelagia is simply permitting herself to join in and have some fun.'

One person who made a particular impression on Penélope during the making of the film was director John Madden. 'He has many great qualities – not just as a director,' she says. 'He's a very wise man – one of the wisest I've met in my life. He's not one of those people

who treats some people good and others bad. He's generous with everybody – treats everyone with respect. And I think this is reflected in his work. As a director, he was a huge inspiration for us because, although he doesn't talk much, everything he gives you is like treasure. I hope I will work with him again.'

Iannis and Pelagia discuss how to treat Mandras's injuries

Penélope began acting in her home city of Madrid, Spain, at the age of fifteen and, two years later, achieved overnight fame in Bigas Luna's film *Jamón, Jamón,* which earned her a Goya nomination, the Spanish equivalent of the Oscar, for Best New Actress. After starring in more than fifteen films in Spain, she was seen in her first English-language film in 1998 in Stephen Frears's *The Hi-Lo Country,* which co-starred Woody Harrelson. This was followed by *Blow,* opposite Johnny Depp, and *All The Pretty Horses,* opposite Matt Damon.

Despite her achievements, Penélope remains unaffected by her success, is friendly, relaxed, has a natural ease with people, and has not lost her enthusiasm for the work. 'I get very excited about it and don't want to lose that. When I feel like that, I feel like a child again and don't want it to stop,' she says.

She is currently being tipped as one of Hollywood's brightest new stars, and her performance in *Captain Corelli's Mandolin* can only add to that. She is not, however, planning to desert Spain or her Spanish roots. She is also widely considered to be one of the world's most beautiful women, but that is not something she dwells upon. 'I am happy with myself, but don't think of myself in that way,' she declares. 'I'm just glad I have a physique that I can change a lot. In the film *Lifeless,* for example, I played a pregnant prostitute who had a row of black teeth and a moustache, and I loved being that character. I enjoy roles where I do not have to look good all the time.'

John Hurt as Doctor Iannis

When it came to John Hurt deciding whether or not he wanted to play Doctor Iannis in *Captain Corelli's Mandolin,* it was not so much a question of where or when Iannis lived that interested John Hurt, but the character of the man.

'His circumstances are of little interest to me,' John explains. 'It is what the man *is* that makes him an attractive person to play. He's been called a hero, but I wouldn't say he was heroic. I think he is a highly scrupulous and enlightened individual. He's something of a seer in the Greek sense of the word, seems to have an understanding of what the island of Cephallonia is, where it is going, what is going to happen and why things are dangerous. He's a kind of doorway for the audience to enter into the story.'

Before starting work on the film John made a conscious decision not to read Louis de Bernières' book, choosing instead to take his direction and understanding of the story from Shawn Slovo's screenplay.

'I never read the book of the film before I do a film because, by its very nature, a film draws on a completely different language. As far as I am concerned the script is, in a sense, the springboard to any part. Even if you are playing someone who is alive – or has lived – and I have done quite a few of

John Hurt describes Iannis as an 'enlightened individual'

those, you still have to treat it as a drama and the same rules apply. I think you can overload your mind with peripheral information that is not much use, and can actually be destructive to the clarity of mind in which you are trying to approach a character.'

John Hurt is, however, confident that the millions who have read de Bernières' novel will be content with the way it has been translated into a film.

'Hopefully the essence of the story remains because both the novel and the film have the same roots and, therefore, the same cumulative effect in terms of the spirit of the piece,' he says. 'Things have to change when a book becomes a film because you don't have two chapters to describe someone's feelings. It has to be told in a more essentially narrative way, and an image on the screen is very different from pages of description.'

No one can accuse actor John Hurt of not taking his acting seriously because his attention to detail is quite extraordinary. Growing a moustache for the role was a simple task that took a month, but the gold tooth decided on for the character required three trips to the dentist.

Dr Iannis examining the pea he has extracted from Stamatis's ear

'This was make-up supervisor Lois Burwell's idea and I jumped on it,' smiles John. 'I love those little touches and thought it was a brilliant idea. It was a very period Greek and Mediterranean thing that seemed just right.'

Some of the spirit of Cephallonia seems to have rubbed off on John. Away from the cameras he appears to be a good decade younger than his sixty years, and his energy is apparent for all to see, as is his sense of adventure. He shunned a chauffeur-driven car to bring him to the set, preferring to travel the seven, sometimes hazardous, miles from his rented home in Aghia Efimia to Dihalia, on a hired moped.

John made his first film, *The Wild and The Willing,* in 1962 and since then has given memorable performances in more than fifty films including *10 Rillington Place, Midnight Express* (for which he won a Golden Globe and a BAFTA as Best Supporting Actor and received an Oscar nomination), *Alien, The Elephant Man* (for which he won a BAFTA and gained an Oscar nomination as Best Actor), *Champions, The Hit, 1984, White Mischief, Scandal, The Field* and *Rob Roy.*

Home for him is Ireland, but he says he felt at home in Cephallonia – perhaps because the Cephallonians remind him of the Irish.

'Neither it seems to me believe in rehearsal,' he smiles. 'Life is there to be grabbed by both horns. I absolutely *love* Cephallonia. It is a fantastic island, and the more you get inside it and get to know the people, the more you discover what a fascinating place it is.'

Christian Bale as Mandras

Christian Bale knew he would have to perfect an authentic Greek accent to play Mandras in *Captain Corelli's Mandolin,* and it was something he enjoyed, probably because he is so good at it. Sounding different, he says, helps him to build a character. He did not, however, realize that he would also have to learn how to handle a boat so proficiently in just a few hours of training that it would look as if he had been sailing all his life.

'It was not something I had quite appreciated I was going to have to do,' he smiles. 'It's not that difficult, but I did hold up a few takes. The fishing was more difficult than you would think, as you are actually attempting to throw a net in a perfect circle. A lot of locals tried to help me learn this art, but one would show me one method, while another would suggest a different way. In the end, I found one that worked for me, which was a hybrid of all their different styles.

'By the end, I got it looking good and would go out to sea thinking I would actually be able to catch some fish, take them home and cook them that evening. I could see hundreds of fish just under the water, and I would think: "This is it . . ." So I'd throw my net, but it would come back up with . . . nothing. The only thing I ever caught was a couple of jellyfish – and that is only because they are so slow!'

It is apparent that Christian is fond of his character, Mandras. 'He goes from being a boy, to becoming a man in the movie and he's a far happier boy than he is a man,' he says. 'He's not educated, but he's somebody who lives and works very much in harmony with nature and lives a pretty simple idyllic life. He knows everybody in his town, but has dreams and aspirations. He thinks that by going away and fighting for his country he will become the man he knows he can be and wants to be for Pelagia, whom he loves, and for the whole town where he wants to be loved and respected by everybody and spend the rest of his life there.

'There's a simplicity about him – about what he wants. Everything is very black and white, but the fact is he has not had any communication with the world or any particular experience of it. So the town is his world, and he loves the place where he was born and wants to die there as well. He loves the people around him, and that's what makes him happy.

'So, in many ways, he's smart because he knows what makes him happy and that's what he is fighting for when he heads off to the war. The trouble is he naively believes that neither village nor anything else will change. He thinks he can go away and fight and then come back and everything, except him, will be exactly the same. He thinks he will be a hero who everyone will love, but that is not what happens. When he returns, everything has changed and the woman he loves is not in love with him any more. So he loses everything . . . He no longer has a home or any of the things that once bought him happiness.'

Mandras may be fictional, but there were many real-life partisans fighting in Cephallonia during the Second World War

Christian, who was born in Wales, made his film début in 1987 at the age of thirteen in Steven Spielberg's film *Empire of the Sun*. For this, he won critical acclaim and an American National Film Board award. Since then he has demonstrated his versatility in a variety of roles in films, which include Kenneth Branagh's *Henry V, Treasure Island, Little Women, Portrait of a Lady, Velvet Goldmine, Metroland, A Midsummer Night's Dream, Shaft* and the controversial *American Psycho*.

Christian knew nothing about the real-life massacre of the Acqui Division on Cephallonia before beginning work on *Captain Corelli's Mandolin*, but working on the film has given him some insight into what happened. More particularly, he now feels he has more understanding of the sacrifices and difficulties faced by the Greek partisans.

'When we were doing the scene where the partisans ambush the German convoys, I gained an insight into the hardships they must have gone through,' he says. 'There was myself, Emelios and Nikos [who play Mandras's fellow partisans, Demetri and Speros] and the rest of the partisans. We had to *really* run up the hills with the gun and it was *exhausting*. It was hot, too, but, because the partisans had worn thick clothes because it was freezing cold at night and in some regions even snowed, so did we for realism. But, obviously – unlike us – they did not have much time to shower or change their clothes, and had to sleep in their clothes all of the time. Perhaps, occasionally, a villager would have let them in to wash or whatever, but that would have been very rare.

'All of the research pictures show the partisans with beards and long hair, and they look as if they've had the same clothes on for a number of weeks. We did the scenes with stuck-on beards, which wasn't very pleasant or comfortable because it felt as if we had glue all over our face the whole time. We also wore army-issue trousers, which were the incredibly scratchy woollen kind. So playing a partisan in *Captain Corelli's Mandolin* was not at all luxurious.'

Irene Papas as Drosoula

Irene Papas had more understanding about the hardships of people living in wartime occupied Greece than most people working on *Captain Corelli's Mandolin*, because she had her own experience of this in childhood. When the war broke out, her parents moved their four daughters from Athens to a small village just a few hours' drive away. Food was short in the capital and they thought they would be able to provide better for their family in the countryside.

'We grew potatoes and other vegetables in the garden, and my mother, who was a teacher, gave lessons to local children who brought her a few things, such as artichokes,' Irene recalls. 'And just like Iannis in the film, we had soldiers billeted in our house, but both Germans and Italians.

'I remember one big difference between a lot of the Germans and the Italians. The Germans would cook their food in a big cauldron and then, afterwards, throw whatever was left on to the ground, although one of them would sometimes give us eggs. The Italians were very different, very gentle with people. There was a particular captain who would give us macaroni, spaghetti and rice. That's why, after they split with the Germans, many Greeks hid the Italians and many Greek girls fell in love with them and married them.'

Drosoula and Pelagia watch as their loved ones depart for war

Iannis and Drosoula
watch as Pelagia and
Mandras dance at their
betrothal

In the novel *Captain Corelli's Mandolin*, de Bernières makes a great play of Drosoula's ugliness, but that was not a part of the character that the film-makers felt it necessary to carry into the film. Irene, now in her seventies, is one of Greece's greatest actresses, has starred in more than sixty films, including the international successes *Anne of the Thousand Days* and *The Guns of Navarone*, and is still a striking-looking woman.

She decided to accept the role of Drosoula, but only after she had ascertained that the film script would not follow de Bernières's controversial depiction of the Greek partisans.

'Knowing the historical truth, I could not have accepted the part if de Bernières's version of the partisans' actions was in the film,' she says. 'It's not because I'm a hero or anything like that, but simply because sometimes you just cannot take part in a lie.'

Irene believes that her character, Drosoula, is devoted to her son Mandras – and that is how she portrays her in the film.

'Drosoula has nothing else in her life but Mandras,' she says, 'so their relationship – although rough on the outside – is very close, very tender. I don't think she is really a hard woman. She is actually very gentle, and that is why she behaves as she does. When you are tender, you sometimes hit out because you are scared; and when you are shy, you shout. Deep down, Drosoula loves Mandras more than anything else in the world.'

Piero Maggio as Carlo

The part of Carlo – the huge, battle-hardened soldier who sacrifices his life to save that of his friend Antonio Corelli – was a very important part to cast in *Captain Corelli's Mandolin*. Carlo *had* to have the right qualities: strong but gentle, tough but thoughtful. Piero Maggio, a burly 6-foot 2-inch man, is perfect for the role. He was a boxer for ten years before going to drama school in Rome to train as an actor, and is also a softly spoken, thoughtful, gregarious individual.

Before he was cast for the film, Piero's English was not good. Casting director Mary Selway, however, thought he had the right look for the film and encouraged him to improve his English, telling him that this would boost his chances of getting the role.

'I told her I'd learn English, and I did,' he smiles. 'For some months I had lessons and talked to as many English and Americans as I could. By the time of the next audition my English was much better. Working on the film helped, too, and by the time I left Cephallonia I could understand most of the things that were said and this made me very happy. Now I would like to be able to speak English as well as I speak Italian – or even better!'

He was delighted that his lessons paid off and he won the role.

'My character, Carlo, is a very strong man,' he says. 'He doesn't speak a lot, but he's very sensitive. He cares for Corelli and his friends in La Scala – thinks of them as brothers. He's fought in Albania, so he's the only one of them who has been to war before and feels he should look after them.'

Piero is just starting out on his acting career and says that working on *Captain Corelli's Mandolin* has helped him enormously. 'I've learned a lot from working with Nick Cage,' he says. 'He's very professional – and I admired that a lot. He worked very hard and I could really believe that he was Captain Corelli and, because of that, could believe I was Carlo. Every actor in the film was very good, so for me filming was like three months at drama school. It was also great for me to have been cast as a

Carlo arrives at the
Italian encampment on
Cephallonia

sensitive man because, normally in Italy, when casting directors see my face and body they think of me for hard-man parts. Hopefully, this film will help to change that.'

While shooting the battle of Argostoli, Piero broke his wrist in a fall and was given a lightweight plaster cast, which he could take off during filming.

'My wrist was a problem for about three weeks,' he says. 'But while I was filming I never felt any real pain. It was only after John Madden said: "Cut!"that I felt any pain. That was because during the actual filming I was too busy thinking about what I was doing. I was concentrating – trying to do my best.'

In real life, Piero has a family connection with the war, which helped him, in an emotional sense, to play the role.

'During the war, a great-uncle of mine was in the Julia Division, which Carlo was in before he joined the Acqui Division,' he says. 'My uncle was later captured and sent to Russia, where he died, we presume, in a prisoner-of-war camp. I had heard about him since I was a child, when my grandmother and grandfather told me about him and were very sad. Thinking about him helped me to empathize in a melancholic way with Carlo in this movie. Doing this film is like a present for my grandparents, who are both now dead, because it helps to tell a story that is largely unknown.'

Piero kept his great-uncle's last letter home in his uniform pocket while filming *Corelli*; and, while in Cephallonia, he visited some of the sites where the Italian troop were massacred.

'I felt very sad about what happened,' he says. 'So many young men were killed. All war is bad, but this massacre was particularly poignant. These men had surrendered, had given up their weapons and thought they would be sent home. Seeing the places where it happened – and hearing about the events – was very powerful. On such a beautiful island, it is hard to imagine such barbarity.'

CAPTAIN CORELLI'S MANDOLIN

David Morrissey as Günter Weber

David Morrissey had always hoped he would land a part in a film of *Captain Corelli's Mandolin*. He had read the book when it first came out in hardback, enjoyed it and anticipated that one day it would be adapted for the big screen. Yet the part he now plays in the film is not the character he first thought might suit him.

'When I heard they were doing the film I thought the role of the British Special Operations Executive man, Bunny Warren, would be a good part for me,' he says. 'But, of course, that character in the book is not in the film.'

David – one of Britain's foremost young acting talents whose previous credits include the television dramas *Holding On*, *Out of the Blue*, *Pure Wickedness*, *Our Mutual Friend* and *The One that Got Away*, together with the films *Hilary and Jackie*, *Born Romantic* and *The Suicide Club* – continues: 'I was asked to screen-test for Weber, so I re-read the sections involving him in the book, read the script and went for the interview. I was delighted to be called in and crossed my fingers that I'd get the role – and it all worked out for me.'

Wearing a thick woollen German army uniform in the forty-plus degree Celsius heat of Cephallonia was a test for David, but one he relished.

La Scala are keen to take up Captain Weber's offer of cigarettes

'I felt very uncomfortable, but that was great because I wasn't there to look sophisticated or cool,' he says. 'I was there to look as if I wasn't relaxed, so standing in the heat was something I indulged in. I wasn't worried about sweating or looking uncomfortable because that's how Weber feels most of the time, both mentally and physically.'

Naturally David, who read books about the Hitler Youth and the rise of Fascism, and watched the acclaimed BBC Television documentary series *Nazis: A Warning From History*, to research his role, has his own views about his character.

'I think Weber is a very confused man,' he says. 'When we meet him, he's certainly not his natural self. He is absolutely in the wrong job, but at the same time he believes – as did the vast majority of Germans at that time – in the Fascist ideal, as it is presented to him. I don't think he has the sophistication to go through the arguments of Fascism with a fine toothcomb and see how repellent it is, but, again, neither did most of his countrymen and women.

'He is essentially, though, a proud good man, with a great love of music, who has never been in any position of authority before and has previously led a pretty sheltered life. He loves spending time with Corelli and the La Scala boys, begins to open up as an emotional person, and starts to learn more about himself.

'The tragedy is that, just as things are going well for him and he is beginning to become a fully rounded person through seeing Corelli and his love of life, the war comes between them and they have to become enemies again. He is a man who would have been devastated by having to shoot anybody, but particularly these men. For him, this is worse than torture and, afterwards, he simply cannot live with himself, but doesn't have the bravery to commit suicide. So, from that point on, he is in a living hell.'

THE LA SCALA BOYS

*'I suppose that the greatest pleasure lay in encountering the boys of
La Scala. These young Italians had been hand-picked for their beauty,
their charm, and their singing.'*

Louis de Bernières

FEDERICO FIORESI

Federico Fioresi is very pleased that the story of the Acqui Division is being
told in *Captain Corelli's Mandolin* because, he says, the deaths of thousands of
his countrymen on Cephallonia should not be forgotten.

'Even when we studied history at school we did not really learn about it,' says
the twenty-eight-year-old. 'We knew it happened, but not in any detail. There
are roads named after military divisions, but nobody really knows the significance
of these. Now, perhaps, people will think more about what happened.

'In the film we portray these boys, who, up until the battle, are singing,
laughing and full of life. Then there is the battle, then the massacre, and people
are certain to be upset by what happens. Perhaps this will make them reflect on
the absurdity of war.'

SANDRO STEFANINI

Tuscany-born Sandro Stefanini, aged twenty-five, knew little about what
happened to his countrymen on Cephallonia during the Second World War, but
made sure he read up as much as he could while on the island.

'I read some articles given to me by members of the production team and
an interview with an Italian soldier,' says Sandro, who is making his film début
in *Captain Corelli's Mandolin*. 'The fate of these men is not well known in Italy,
so I am glad the film is telling their story. My grandfather fought in Albania
and was in Greece for twenty days, but he didn't know much about what
happened in Cephallonia.'

Sandro's favourite scene is the one where Corelli plays Pelagia's Song for
the first time outside the *kapheneion*. 'It is a very romantic scene and nearly all
the cast are in it.'

When he did his national service, he chose civil rather than military service.

'I drove an ambulance for ten months,' he says. 'So I had never carried a
gun before I started working on this film.'

(Overleaf) Captain Corelli and La Scala sing along to a record. *Left to right*: Federico Fioresi, Simone Spinazzè, Francesco Guzzo, Paco Reconti, Sergio Albelli, Davide Quatraro, Nicolas Cage, Piero Maggio, Salvatore Lazzaro, Sandro Stefanini, Nuccio Siano and Germano di Mattia

FRANCESCO GUZZO

Before he auditioned for the La Scala role, thirty-one-year-old Francesco Guzzo, a veteran of twenty Italian films, admits he knew nothing about *Captain Corelli's Mandolin* or the real-life fate of the Acqui Division during the war.

'I was very pleased to get a part in the film, and it was the first time I had worked outside Italy,' says Francesco, who comes from Palermo, Sicily. 'I only knew a couple of the other Italian actors before starting on the film, but all of us, despite being very different people, got on well and found a bond between us, rather like La Scala.

'Perhaps because we all became friends during the first two weeks together, once rehearsals started and we learned how to march and hold guns correctly, we understood how soldiers would have become close – bonded with each other – in wartime.

'That certainly helped me when it came to filming the massacre scene because I was able to visualize us in the same situation. I pushed my own imagination, pictured us there in wartime – and that made it all feel very real. My character is the first soldier to understand that he is going to die, and he falls to his knees and cries. My tears were real tears . . . and it isn't easy to cry like that.'

The Italians celebrate the fall of Mussolini. *Left to right*: Paco Reconti, Francesco Guzzo, Piero Maggio, Sergio Albelli, Federico Fioresi, Davide Quatraro, Germano di Mattia, Sandro Stefanini and Simone Spinazzè

GERMANO DI MATTIA

Germano di Mattia comes from the Italian town of Avezzano, birthplace of General Gandin.

'It was an odd coincidence,' he says. 'But the story of what happened to the Acqui Division is not well known in Italy and I am glad that it is now being told.

'When I first saw the script to *Captain Corelli's Mandolin*, I was very interested and I am glad to be a part of the film. I would have loved to have played Carlo, but I realize I am not the right size for him!'

Germano, who is thirty-two and has been acting for twelve years, says his favourite part of the film is when La Scala are frolicking in the sea with the Italian prostitutes. 'That was fun to film,' he says. 'The scene I enjoyed least was the massacre scene – it was a very disturbing experience.'

As he had done military national service, Germano did have some experience of handling weapons before starting work on the film. But he says: 'During my military service, I was stationed near France and my actual job was to organize the General's holidays. I learned to ski, played music, sang and had a good time!'

SIMONE SPINAZZÈ

When the Italian soldiers hear that Mussolini has fallen, they think they are now going to be able to go home, and there is much happiness and celebrating. So much so, that one La Scala man even kisses an old lady.

'I had to kiss and hug this old-lady extra,' laughs twenty-eight-year-old Rome-born Simone Spinazzè. 'It was a really deep kiss and she was a lovely woman who gave off a lot of light. The film is full of fantastic actors and John Madden is a very special director.'

SERGIO ALBELLI

Despite the fact that he had never really sung before, thirty-five-year-old Sergio Albelli, who was born in Serravalle Pistolese, Tuscany, but now lives in Rome, enjoyed singing in *Captain Corelli's Mandolin* most of all.

'Singing in front of other people for the first time was a great experience,' he says. 'Their reaction was really good and I was incredibly surprised by how much a song could touch people.'

He was also very impressed by director John Madden. 'He has a huge quantity of positive energy which he puts into his work, and then all the people around him want to do their best. He can get a good performance from people without creating any pressure at all.'

DAVIDE QUATRARO

At twenty-three years old, Davide Quatraro is the youngest member of La Scala and the only one, other than Corelli and Carlo, who actually has a name in the film.

'My character is called Piero, and this is revealed when Corelli introduces La Scala to Captain Weber and describes Carlo as "a semi-quaver",' says Davide, who comes from southern Italy.

Captain Corelli's Mandolin is Davide's first film and he enjoyed every minute of the filming.

'It's been a great experience, I have learned a great deal from Nick and from everyone, including John Madden and my colleagues in La Scala.'

But whereas some of his colleagues say that the massacre scene was their least favourite, Davide has a different view.

'As an actor I think it's important to be able to die well – and it is something I have always wanted to do,' he says. 'I did a lot of things for this film that I like to do, such as dying, singing, dancing and swimming. I was supposed to have a stunt double for my death, but in rehearsals the stunt co-ordinator decided I could do it myself.

'I was very proud of that. We rehearsed on mats, but when we filmed the scene I had to be shot while I was trying to run away and escape. I was shot in the back and, even though I had kneepads on, I bruised my legs. We had to shoot the scene many, many times from lots of different angles.'

PACO RECONTI

At forty, Paco Reconti, who hails from Reggio Calabria in southern Italy, is the oldest member of La Scala.

'I was a parachutist,' he says. 'As I had to spend a year doing my National Service, I thought I should not waste the opportunity and chose, therefore, to do something memorable. I volunteered to be a parachutist and it was great.'

Paco has a family connection with another German wartime atrocity. In March 1944, Italian partisans exploded a bomb in Rome which killed twenty-eight German SS troops on their daily march, and the German response was swift. On Hitler's orders they snatched civilians from the street and took them to a nearby network of caves where they slaughtered 335 local people. Paco's mother's cousin was on his way home from his office job when he was arrested by the Germans and became one of their victims.

NUCCIO SIANO

Nuccio Siano is the member of La Scala who plays the guitar in both the party scene and the key mandolin scene.

'I enjoyed those two scenes because they are recognizable roles for me,' says the thirty-nine-year-old from Salerno.

However, like many of his colleagues, he found the massacre scene the most memorable moment. 'It was filmed with six cameras and was a very moving and impressive experience,' he says. 'It was quite realistic. There were Germans firing at us and blood exploding from our shirts.'

Nuccio has a family connection with Cephallonia: his uncle was a survivor of the massacre. 'My uncle was in the army and, having survived the Germans, was then taken prisoner by the English and brought to England where he spent a few years.'

SALVATORE LAZZARO

Every actor playing a member of La Scala gets to say one line in the film and Salvatore Lazzaro, who comes from Catania in Sicily, particularly enjoyed his moment. 'My line came just before Captain Corelli plays Pelagia's Song for the first time,' says twenty-nine-year-old Salvatore.

'I had to say: "It's a beautiful night and everything is peaceful and we should think about falling in love . . ." and it was great to have a line in such an atmospheric and memorable scene in the movie.

'I was very happy to be in the film. The story of what happened to the Italians on Cephallonia is almost unknown and I think it was very important that more people know about the tragedy. I am very pleased that the story is now being told.'

φ φ φ φ φ

There wasn't a member of the cast who was not affected by the true-life story of the slaughter of thousands of young Italian soldiers on Cephallonia during the Second World War. So, instead of the shoot becoming a unique experience in which the actors spent four months in a breathtakingly beautiful location creating just another piece of cinematic entertainment, the making of the film became an episode in their lives that they will remember forever. It was also one that makes nonsense of the expression 'All is fair in love and war', because as *Captain Corelli's Mandolin* proves, nothing, in fact, is fair in either.

Chapter 8
AN ISLAND IN HISTORY

*Cephallonia, the largest of the Ionian Islands and the third
largest Greek island, is situated at the outlet of the Patraicos Gulf,
between the islands of Zakynthos and Levkada. The Ionian
Islands' strategic maritime location between the Italian and
Greek mainlands has meant that, throughout history, they
have attracted the envious eye of great powers in need of ports
and supplies, or, in some cases, simply as part of
their expansionist empires.*

'The half-forgotten island of Cephallonia rises improvidently and inadvisedly from the Ionian Sea; it is an island so immense in antiquity that the very rocks themselves exhale nostalgia and the red earth lies stupefied not only by the sun, but also by the impossible weight of memory.'

So wrote Dr Iannis in his unfinished *The New History of Cephallonia* in *Captain Corelli's Mandolin*. But the island might not be so forgotten any more. In fact, these days, it has become one of the most popular tourist destinations in Greece. Obviously it is impossible to say just how many extra visitors the island has attracted since the book, *Captain Corelli's Mandolin*, was first published in 1994, but, sitting in the departure lounge of Kefallinia airport, you do not have to look far before you spot somebody carrying or reading the novel, and for those who have not brought one with them, the airport shop sells copies.

The impact of John Madden's film, *Captain Corelli's Mandolin*, will boost the number of visitors still further – a blessing to some of the islanders, an unwanted intrusion to others. What the visitors will discover is just over 300 square miles of island, which, outside its bustling main town of Argostoli and smaller towns of Lixouri, Poros and Sami, is largely unspoiled and sparsely developed.

Cephallonia, the largest of the Ionian Islands and the third largest Greek island, has as its own geographical focal point Mount Aenos, which looms 1,628 metres high, and also some truly stunning beaches – including the crescent-shaped Myrtos beach, which is one of the most beautiful in the region, if not in Greece itself. Cephallonia is also situated close to a geographical fault

Modern-day
Cephallonia: a view of
the beautiful town of
Assos

line, which has led to some cataclysmic earthquakes throughout its history and minor tremors are not uncommon.

When, in de Bernières' book, Antonio Corelli returns, as an old man, to Cephallonia in October 1993, he remarks: 'Everything here used to be so pretty and now everything is concrete.' He is, however, being a little harsh on the island. If you take a turning off one of the main routes, which links its towns, it is very easy to find yourself alone on an unsealed track.

The island's mountainous terrain is a challenge for two-wheel drive cars and walkers alike, but it is certainly worth exploring some of the heights because any peak on Cephallonia offers the traveller remarkable views across the island and, depending on your location, out to sea.

Standing there in the silence – apart, that is, from the distant tinkle of goats' bells – presents the perfect opportunity to reflect on the island's history. The mountains themselves – so massive, solid and immovable, like the island itself – have seen so much, yet remain constant, a line of continuity through an often troubled history.

Cephallonia is situated at the outlet of the Patraicos Gulf, between the islands of Zakynthos and Levkada. The Ionian Islands strategic maritime

In *Corelli*, local people were recruited as extras (above) and (right) the body of the saint is carried during the feast of St Gerasimos

(Opposite) A nineteenth-century engraving of Cephallonia

CAPTAIN CORELLI'S MANDOLIN

10,000 BC:
First indications
of settlers on
Cephallonia.

1900 to 1100 BC:
Cephallonia becomes a
thriving trading post.

700 BC:
The island is ruled
from four great
autonomous cities.

187 BC:
Romans land on
Cephallonia and
occupy it.

1185 to 394 BC:
The Byzantine era.

AD 1084:
Normans unsuccessfully
try to take the island.

AD 1479:
The Turks take
the island.

AD 1504:
Venetian rule begins.

AD 1538:
Pirate Barbarossa
attacks and takes
13,000 people as slaves.

AD 1636:
Earthquake hits
the island and kills
540 people.

AD 1640:
Civil unrest and uprising
breaks out.

location between the Italian and Greek mainlands has meant that, throughout history, they have attracted the envious eye of great powers in need of ports and supplies, or, in some cases, simply as part of their expansionist empires.

Cephallonia is believed to be one of the first parts of Greece to have been inhabited, and fossils and bones, which were found in Fiskardo, date back to at least 10,000 BC and possibly as early as 50,000 BC. These remains are thought to be those of nomadic hunters who would have travelled to Cephallonia and other islands in the region in search of food. There is also some evidence from the archaeological finds that the nomads also began to settle on the island.

By the Bronze Age BC there were definitely organized settlements on Cephallonia. During the Mycenaean period (1900–1100 BC), the time of the first great civilization on the Greek mainland, the island thrived and became a major trading post.

By 700 BC, the island was divided into four great cities Pale, Same (modern-day Sami), Kranea (which stood where Argostoli is now) and Proni. Each of these fortified cities, of which some remains can still be seen, was autonomous, issued its own coinage and made its own allies. Relations between the four were not always cordial, however. Even though they all worshipped the same Olympian gods and were at times united against a common enemy, such as the Persians, at other times, during the Peloponnesian War (431–404 BC) – which was fought between the two pre-eminent city-states in ancient Greece, Athens and Sparta – they were divided.

In 187 BC, Cephallonia was occupied by the Romans, but only after the people of Same had withstood a siege lasting four months.

Then, with the downfall of the Roman Republic in the fifth century,
Cephallonia, along with sixty-four other provinces and 935 cities, was ruled
by the Byzantine Empire, which had survived the fall of the rest of the Roman
empire in the West. Byzantine hegemony lasted for five centuries before
Norman adventurer Robert Guiscard – who gave his name to the town of
Fiskardo – attempted to occupy the island, in 1084. He was defeated by the
Cephallonians at Pale, but a century later his descendants managed to take the
island, only for it later to come under the control of the pirate Matteo Orsini.
He and his descendants ruled for 150 years before they were succeeded by the
Tokos dynasty in 1357.

Following a two-decade spell under Turkish rule, which began in 1479,
during which many of the island's inhabitants fled to escape the harsh regime,
in 1504 Cephallonia came under Venetian rule, which lasted nearly 300 years.
The island became an important port for the Venetian fleet but still came under
sporadic attack from Turkish pirates including the legendary Barbarossa, who
in 1538 raided the island and carried off 13,000 people to be sold as slaves.

Under control from Venice, the local population lived meagre existences
compared to those of their rulers. In 1640, four years after an earthquake which

killed 540 people, civil war broke out among the nobility, peasants and farmers which continued for some years. A subsequent earthquake in 1658 destroyed Lixouri and cost more than 300 lives. Despite such events, the island flourished through trade, and its population increased at around this time to 70,000 with incomers from Venice, mainland Greece and the Peloponnese moving to the island.

By the early eighteenth century Venetian power had begun to decline, and, on 1 May 1797, French leader Napoleon Bonaparte declared war on Venice and, a matter of weeks later, French forces occupied Cephallonia.

The French set about trying to improve the Cephallonians' educational and intellectual life by founding schools and libraries. However, just a year later, following the British Admiral Nelson's defeat of the French fleet at the Battle of the Nile, Britain let Russia and Turkey take control of the Ionian Islands. Under the Treaty of Constantinople of March 1800, a new semi-autonomous Ionian state was founded. In 1802, popular elections were held and the following year a new constitution was created and Greek was confirmed as the official language.

Four years later, Cephallonia and the other Ionian Islands once again came under French control via that country's treaty with Russia and were officially declared part of the French Empire. However, within two years, the British took possession in a bloodless invasion – and the following year a new British commander, a Swiss, Major Philipe de Bosset, became Governor.

In November 1815, a few months after the Battle of Waterloo, Cephallonia and the other islands were made a British protectorate under the name of The United States of the Ionian Islands. Then, following the establishment of

AD 1656:
Lixouri destroyed by an earthquake. 300 dead.

AD 1757:
Argostoli becomes the capital of Cephallonia.

AD 1767:
An earthquake on the island costs 253 lives.

AD 1797:
France occupies Cephallonia.

AD 1798:
The French withdraw, the Turks and Russians arrive.

AD 1800:
Semi-autonomous Ionian state founded.

AD 1801:
Russian forces leave.

AD 1803:
Greek becomes the official language on Cephallonia.

AD 1807:
The French regain control.

AD 1809:
British rule begins.

AD 1815:
The Ionian Islands are declared a British protectorate.

Ο ΑΓΙΟΣ

ΓΕΡΑ
ΣΙ
ΜΟ
Σ
Ο ΕΝ
ΚΕΦΑΛΛΗΝΙΑ

ΙC ΧC
ΝΙΚΑ

«ΤΕΚΝΙΑ ΕΙ
ΡΗΝΕΥΕΤΕ ΕΝ
ΕΑΤΟΙΣ ΚΑΙ
ΜΗ ΤΑ ΥΨΗ
ΛΑ ΦΡΟΝΕΙ
ΤΕ.»

A view over Argostoli showing Drapano bridge

AD 1864:
Cephallonia and the
Ionian Islands are ceded
to Greece.

AD 1867:
Earthquake hits the
western side
of Cephallonia –
224 die.

30 April 1941:
Italian paratroops land
on Cephallonia.

31 April 1941:
Italy's full-invasion force
arrives.

August 1943:
German forces arrive
on Cephallonia.

13 September 1943:
Italian forces on
Cephallonia attack
German reinforcements.

22 September 1943:
Italian forces surrender
to the Germans, and the
massacre of the
prisoners begins.

10 September 1944:
German forces withdraw
from Cephallonia.

9 August 1953:
Earthquake devastates
much of Cephallonia,
killing more than
600 people.

independent Greece in 1829 as a monarchy under Otto I, there was an increasing desire among the Ionian islanders to form a union with the mainland. The British – although granting certain liberties, such as the freedom of the press and increasing the powers of local representation – did not act fast enough for the islanders; and, in September 1848, there was an uprising on Cephallonia with locals meeting the British army on Drapano bridge.

On 23 September 1863, the Ionian Parliament voted in favour of a union with the rest of Greece, the British finally agreed, and on 21 May 1864 the islands were formally ceded to Greece.

Having finally been freed from a succession of rulers of different nationalities, the population of Cephallonia could have been forgiven for expecting that, perhaps, after more than two millennia under the rule of others, they were finally free to enjoy self-determination. Following the Union with Greece, they did for nearly eighty years. However, in 1941 the island was invaded once again, this time by Italian and then subsequently German forces.

The German occupation lasted until 10 September 1944, and was marked by the constant and valiant resistance of Greek partisan groups. But any success by their freedom fighters was met with violent reprisals from the invaders.

In the latter years of the war, there were skirmishes between Royalist EDES and the Communist EAM-ELAS guerrillas and, following the German withdrawal from Greece, these erupted into full-scale fighting which lasted,

(Opposite) An icon of St Gerasimos, patron saint of Cephallonia

AN ISLAND IN HISTORY

A Cephallonian woman stands among the debris in the recreation of the 1953 earthquake

The real earthquake destroyed much of the island and killed more than 600 people

off and on – despite international efforts from Britain and the United States – until the beginning of the 1950s. This civil war was marked by brutality on both sides and, to this day, remains a dark period of Greek history.

Between 9 and 14 August 1953 a succession of 113 tremors and aftershocks reduced a large number of Cephallonia's towns and villages to rubble. More than 600 islanders died and Argostoli, with its beautiful Venetian architecture, was reduced to rubble.

Even while filming was still taking place, enterprising postcard companies began producing views of the set

The devastation was almost total, with an estimated seventy per cent of the island's buildings ruined. Many villages were simply abandoned, but towns like Argostoli and Sami were gradually rebuilt, although sadly not with any serious regard for recreating its glorious architectural past.

However, not for the first time in its long history, Cephallonia and its people rose again from the dust of destruction and the modern island is a thriving place with almost 28,000 inhabitants. Perhaps reflecting their ancestors' need to constantly adapt to incomers, today's Cephallonians remain a welcoming, adaptable and open people.

Cephallonia is a relaxed island, seemingly unfazed by events, able to renew and grow again – a place with a sense that whatever history throws at it, and whatever circumstances its people find themselves in, they – like the island itself – will survive. Both, after all, have already proved this time and time again.

So, thanks to Louis de Bernières' book, *Captain Corelli's Mandolin*, a forgotten part of Cephallonia's Second World War history has now been revealed. And, as I finish writing this film-companion book, the sets for *Captain Corelli's Mandolin* are being dismantled, the cast of actors are scattering to other parts of the globe, and the production team is back in London planning its next project. The islanders – all those who, for a brief while, shared in the making of the film – are settling down again into the post-script, post-film life of Cephallonia, and the invasion of tourists that this has attracted.

To most Cephallonians this new influx of outsiders is to be welcomed. However, there are some who worry about how the island has been and will be changed to accommodate them. But then Cephallonia has always been a place where adapting to new circumstances is something to be taken in its stride, and at least these new twenty-first-century visitors arrive with no malevolent intent and simply come in search of sun, sea and sand – and for many of them a chance to discover a little of the magic of *Captain Corelli's Mandolin*.

Cast and crew list

CAST

Captain Antonio Corelli	Nicolas Cage
Pelagia	Penélope Cruz
Dr Iannis	John Hurt
Mandras	Christian Bale
Captain Weber	David Morrissey
Drosoula	Irene Papas
Carlo	Piero Maggio
Stamatis	Gerasimos Skiadaresis
Mrs Stamatis	Aspasia Kralli
Kokolios	Michalis Giannatos
Father Arsenios	Dimitris Kamperidis
Velisarios	Pedro Sarubi
Lemoni (6 years)	Joanna-Daria Adraktas
General Gandin	Roberto Citran
Colonel Barge	Patrick Malahide
The Soldiers of La Scala	Federico Fioresi
	Sandro Stefanini
	Francesco Guzzo
	Germano di Mattia
	Simone Spinazzè
	Sergio Albelli
	Davide Quatraro
	Paco Reconti
	Nuccio Siano
	Salvatore Lazzaro
Eleni	Viki Maragaki
Mayor	George Kotanidis
Italian Quartermaster	Vincent Riotta
The German Commanders	Martin Glyn Murray
	Till Bahlman
	Renny Krupinski
Trembling Man	Kostas Phillipoglou
Nun	Froso Korou
Mad Woman Mina	Alexia Bouloukou
Recruiting Officer	Antonis Antoniou
Mother	Natalia Capo d'Istria
Town Clerk	Tasos Palantzidis
Italian Captain	Massimiliano Pazzaglia
Italian Colonel	Tim Hardy
Dimitris	Emilios Chilakis
Spiros	Nikolas Karathanos
Smoking Italian Soldier	Francesco Cabras
Dancing Italian Soldier	Nunzio Lombardo
Italian Soldier	Sandro Repossi
The Mad People	Maria Louisa Papadopoulou
	Dina Kafterani
	Vlassis Zotis
	Panagiotis Thanassoulis
The Italian Prostitutes	Irene Eleftheriou
	Sofia Yannioti
	Marina Maria Corelli
	Evi Tzortzi

	Leticia Moustaki
	Angelika Lambri
	Maria Philipakopoulou
	Irene Christidi
German Soldier	Peter Stark
Lemoni's Mother	Katerina Didiskalou
Older Lemoni	Ira Tavlaridis
Greek Partisans	Babis Artelaris
	Gerasimos Iakovatos
	Nikos Kalogiratos
	Dionysis Karlis
	Pavlos Lalis
	Angelos Liberatos
	Panagis Polichronatos
	Christos Rangas
	Dimitris Vandoros
	Gerasimos Xidias
Guitar Players	Dimitris Dimoulas
	Pantelis Filipatos
Violin Player	Ilias Theofilatos
Toubeleki Player	Makis Filipatos

CREW

Director	John Madden
Producers	Tim Bevan
	Eric Fellner
	Kevin Loader
	Mark Huffam
Screenplay	Shawn Slovo
Director of Photography	John Toll ASC
Production Designer	Jim Clay
Film Editor	Mick Audsley
Costume Designer	Alexandra Byrne
Music	Stephen Warbeck
Casting Director	Mary Selway
Associate Producer	Susie Tasios
Co-producers	Jane Frazer
	Debra Hayward
	Liza Chasin
Production Supervisor	Kathy Sykes
Unit Production Manager	Nigel Gostelow
1st Assistant Director	Deborah Saban
Sound Recordist	Peter Lindsay
Financial Controller	Andy Hennigan
Location Manager	Elena Restaki
Chief Make-up Artist	Lois Burwell
Chief Hairdresser	Lisa Tomblin
Second Camera/Steadicam Operator	Peter Cavaciuti
Post Production Supervisor	Tania Windsor Blunden
Supervising Sound Editor	John Downer
Rerecording Mixer	Adrian Rhodes
Supervising Art Director	Chris Seagers

Art Director	Gary Freeman	Prosthetics Make-up Supervisor	Connor O'Sullivan
Standby Art Director	Peter Bull	Prosthetics Make-up	Jo Allen
Assistant Art Director	Alan Gilmore	Mr Cage's Make-up	Allen Weisinger
Set Decorator	John Bush	Mr Cage's Hairdresser	Joseph Coscia
Production Buyer	Michael Standish	Make-up Artist	Catherine Heys
Art Department Coordinator	Rea Apostolides	Crowd Make-up Supervisor	Sian Grigg
Graphic Artist	Mina Miraphora	Crowd Make-up Artist	Jennifer Hegarty
Draughtsperson	Rob Cowper	Hairdresser	Elisabetta de Leonardis
Junior Draughtsperson	Heidi Gibb	Crowd Hairdressing Supervisor	Ferdinando Merolla
Décor and Lettering Artist	Steven Hedinger	Costume Supervisor	Sharon Long
Scenic Artist	Steve Mitchell	Assistant Costume Designer	Jane Petrie
Drapes Master	Chris Seddon	Costume Assistant (Italy)	Anna Lombardi
Production Manager	Nikos Nikolettos	Crowd Wardrobe Coordinator	Marion Weise
Assistant Production Manager	Jenny Panoutsopoulou	Wardrobe Master	Anthony Brookman
Production Coordinator	Diane Chittell	Crowd Wardrobe Mistress	Anabel Campbell
Assistant Production Coordinators	Tania Clarke	Costume Department Assistant (UK)	Una Nicholson
	Mary Alexopoulou	Costume Cutter (UK)	Susannah Wilson
	Sevasti Morou Kelly	Assistant Costume Cutter (UK)	Dominic Young
Assistant Location Manager	Paris Karagiorgos	Costume Breakdown	Steve Gell
Accommodation Coordinator	Rita Kassiotis	Military Webbing	Andrew Fletcher
2nd Assistant Directors	Olivia Lloyd	Gaffer	Mick Morris
	Takis Yannopoulos	Best Boy	Matthew Buchan
	Karen Richards	Rigging Gaffer	Gary Hill
	Toby Hefferman	Practical Electrician	George Kavaleratos
3rd Assistant Directors	Benjamin Howard	Property Master	Barry Gibbs
	Dimitris Birbilis	Supervising Dressing Props	Martin Kingsley
	Simos Koroxenidis	Dressing Props Coordinator	Andreas Siroyannis
	Pieros Andrakakos	Chargehand Standby Props	Alfie Smith
Focus Pullers	Chris Toll	Standby Props	Wesley Peppiatt
	Graham Hall		Danny Burke
Clapper Loaders	Ian Coffey		Bill Hargreaves
	Chris Dale	Standby Props Assistant	Makis Defteros
	Alan Hall	Livestock	Paris Burletos
Key Grip	Kenny Atherford	Storeman	Brian West
B Camera Grip	Philip Kenyon	Construction Coordinator	John Bohan
Grip	Paraskevas Grillis	Assistant Construction Coordinator	Tom Martin
Crane Operator	James Folly	Supervising Stagehand	George King
Video Operator	Andrew Haddock	HOD Rigger	Peter Hawkins
Sound Maintenance	Malcolm Rose	Supervising Rigger	Alan Williams
Boom Operator	Nikos Bougioukos	Chargehand Rigger	Ron Meeks
Script Editor	Irena Brignull	Riggers	Keith Carey
Script Supervisor	Kim Armitage		Scott Hillier
Dialect Coach	Joan Washington	Supervising Carpenters	David Lowery
Additional Dialect Coach	Sally Grace		Robert Wishart
1st Assistant Editor	Mags Arnold		Ioannis Baratas
1st Assistant Editor (Film)	Paul Elman		Gary Hedges
2nd Assistant Editor	Aggela Despotidou	Chargehand Carpenters	Danny O'Regan
Assistant Editor (Rushes)	Amy Quince		Martin Freeman
Trainee Assistant Editor	Carmen Morrow		Peter Brown
Dialogue Editor	Sarah Morton	HOD Scenic Painter	Clive Ward
Foley Editors	Mike Feinberg	Supervising Painter	David Haberfield
	Bob Risk	Master Plasterers	Terry James
Additional Sound Editor	Colin Chapman		Dave Coldham
ADR Voice Casting	Louis Elman AMPS	Supervising Plasterer	Peter McCarroll
Key 2nd Make-up Artist	Pauline Heys	Chargehand Plasterer	Nicholas Barringer
Key 2nd Hairdresser	Kay Georgiou	Plasterer	Andrew Tombs

Stonemasons	George Kavaleratos	2nd Assistant Director	Paul Taylor
	Gerassimos Filippatos	3rd Assistant Director	Panagiotis Kravas
SFX Supervisor	Richard Conway	Lighting Cameraman	Peter Field
Senior SFX Technician/Buyer	Michalis Samiotis	Camera Operator	John Palmer
Senior SFX Technicians	Andrew Kelly	Focus Pullers	John Gamble
	Tim Willis		Brad Larner
SFX Technicians	Sam Conway	Clapper Loaders	Robert Palmer
	Nigel Nixon		Simon Sarketzis
	Trevor Butterfield	Grips	Ron Nicholls
	Anthony Richards		Bill Geddes
SFX Wire Rigger	Ceri Nicholls	Script Supervisor	Sharon Mansfield
Casting Director (Greece)	Makis Gazis	Sound Recordist	Thanassis Arvanitis
Casting Director (Italy)	Shaila Ruben	Gaffer	Steve Costello
Extras Casting (Greece)	Stavros Kaplanidis	Standby Props	Clive Wilson
Casting Assistant	Fiona Weir	Visual Effects	Double Negative
Choreographer	Quinny Sacks	Visual Effects Producer	Fay McConkey
Assistant Choreographer	Nunzio Lombardo	Line Producer	Emily Edwards
Stunt Coordinators	Jim Dowdall	Production Assistant	Clare Tinsley
	Marc Cass	Lead 3D Animators	Jake Mengers
Assistant to Stunt Coordinator	Ira Kiourti		Peter Bebb
Marine Coordinator	James Wakeford	Technical Directors	Elie Jamaa
Marine Assistant	Yuri Averof		Julian Mann
Diving Supervisors	Ian Creedy	Software R&D	Martin Preston
	Darren Bailey	Lead Digital Compositor	Simon Terry
Diver/Safety Officer	Lee Murphy	Rotoscope Artists	Ciaran Crowley
Military Technical Advisor	Richard Smedley		Guiliano Dionisio Vigano
Military Advisor in Rome	Giorgio Cantelli	VFX Editorial	John Seymour
Military Trainers	Brian Bosley		James R. Carew
	Ken Williams	Chief Engineer	Ian Chisholm
	Paul Goldsmith	Technical Operations Manager	Steve MacPherson
	Richard Blackburn	Technical Support	Simon Burley
20/20 Coordinator	Ian Dray	Studio Manager	Pete Hanson
Action Vehicles	Plus Film Services	Music Supervisor	Becky Bentham
	Steven Lamonby	Music Editor	Andy Glen
Action Vehicle Coordinator	Hank Schumacher	Assisted by	Tony Lewis
Armoured Vehicle Supervisor	David Carson		James Bellamy
Supervising Armourer	Charlie Bodycomb	Location Musical Director	Paul Englishby
Armourers	Zorg Ltd Film Armourers	Mandolin Coach to Mr Cage	John Parichelli
	Dale Clarke	Music Recorded and Mixed by	Chris Dibble
Unit Publicist	Sarah Clark	Assisted by	Jake Jackson
Stills Photographer	Peter Mountain	Music Conducted by	Nick Ingman
Production Health and Safety Advisor	Alan Sable	Composer's Assistant	Andrew Green
Fireman	Bill Ratty	Music Orchestrated by	Stephen Warbeck
Unit Nurse	Carrie Johnson	Additional Orchestration	Paul Englishby
Paramedic	Brian Bulldock		Andrew Green
Transport Coordinator	Bryan Baverstock		Nick Ingman
Transport Assistant	Ilias Grigoriou	Orchestra Leader	Rolf Wilson
		Songs Arranged by	Paul Englishby

Second Unit

2nd Unit Director	Vic Armstrong
1st Assistant Director	Terry Madden

Developed and produced in association with Free Range Films with special thanks to Roger Michell

Index

Vessels, films and fictional characters are shown in *italic*. References to illustrations are given in **bold**.

PICTURE CREDITS

Adam Editions, Athens: 187
Argostoli Archive: 7
Bundesarchiv, Bild, Koblenz: 26-7 (background), 27, 28, 33 (top)
Steve Clark: 6
Mary Evans Picture Library: 181, 185
Printed Word: 105 (top)
Topham Picturepoint: 186-7 (background), 186 (bottom)